GOLD

As October Sunsets, a
Stray Dog, and God's
Good Plans

LINDA JANE NIEDFELDT

20 Twenty
Literary Group

ISBN
978-1-962868-16-7 (Paperback)
978-1-962868-17-4 (eBook)

GOLD

Acknowledgements

I'd like to acknowledge Lydia Zangl and Erica Borgen (both deceased) for memories shared during the writing of the first two books in the Lisenka series: *RED as in Russia and Measles and Love* and *GREEN as in Springtime, New Life, and God's Will.* These two ladies didn't realize, and neither did I, that they were inadvertently preparing my thoughts to write the third: *WHITE as Christmas Snow, a Candle's Glow, and Heaven's Robe* and the fourth: *GOLD as October Sunsets, a Stray Dog, and God's Good Plans*

Thanks

-to Gloria Pipping, the Brooke Street neighbors, and their friends for sharing memories of life back then

-to Ronnell Gibson for our initial brain-storming session

-to Bonnie Braun for sharing her love of dogs with me and for helping me create an adorable, believable, but fictional golden retriever, Goldy

-to Betty Hall (deceased) and Bonnie Strelow for assistance in my research of the Infant Socks Factory and for demonstrating a stumpf fiddle and to Bonnie for providing a stumpf fiddle for our photo session

-to Jerry King for pointing out the location of another hobo jungle in town and for sharing the sock-stealing incidents at Infant Socks

-to Cindy Boelk and Evelyn McLean-Cowan for their descriptions of historic Fond du Lac, including a policeman walking the beat

-to John and Charmaine Luczak for approving my description of the Infant Socks Factory and for permission to use their last name. John's dad and his uncle were in management positions at Infant Socks. My character Mr. Luczak in the book is neither one, but a bit of each. In the photo of Mr. Luczak, John is sitting at his dad's old desk.

-to the people who served as readers during the progressive stages of the manuscript: Carla Jahnke, Tom Niedfeldt, Carol Kolosovsky, Sondra Retzlaff, Tracy Reinhardt (historical accuracy), and Kristi Scorcio.

-to Carla Jahnke of Carla Jane Photography—FDL for organizational skills, photo illustrations extraordinaire, and computer support (No animals were injured during our photo sessions.)

-to Linda Lueck for providing the historical costumes and props

-to the people who portrayed characters in (somewhat) the order of their appearance: Hannah Witte (Lisenka/Lis), Graham Niedfeldt (Yurgi), Abby Jahnke (Alya), Bryce Jahnke (Jimmy), Alix Jahnke (Marty), Carla Jahnke (Taty/Mama), Caleb Niedfeldt

(Pavel/Papa), Brady Loberger (Max), Carissa Loberger (Hildy), Keith Hellwig (Officer Kowalski), Dale Witte (Eddy Monroe), Jill Niedfeldt (Miss Meuschlin), Anthony Petrowitz (Albert, back view, and Roy), Larry Lamont (Heinrich), Pastor David Haag (Austin), Mason Musack (John), John Luczak (Mr. Luczak)

-to Laurie and Tim Krawczyk for sharing their beautiful golden retriever Blake (Goldy) with us and to Chrissy Krawczyk for handling Blake for the photos.

-to the following for photo settings: Lisa Lefeber and the Fond du Lac County Historical Society—Galloway House and Village, Larry Lamont for his beautiful Willys Knight automobile, Carla and Dan Jahnke for their home scenes and their chicken Ashley (Rosie)

-to my professional and patient editor, bestselling author Liz Tolsma

-to NaNoWriMo (National Novel Writing Month) for the challenge of writing a 50,000 word novel in November

-to God for filling in the story line when I didn't know what was happening next

Introduction

In the mid 1700s, German people migrated into Russia to find a better life. There the German-Russian people lived in peace for more than a hundred years. In the late 1800s, however, the Russian leaders began to take away the Germans' freedom. Life became increasingly hard, but when Stalin gained control of Russia, life became miserable.

The first book in the Lisenka series, *RED as in Russia and Measles and Love*, begins in 1926, while ten-year-old Lisenka and her family are struggling to survive in communist Russia. When Commandant Chukov closes their Christian school, takes their Bible, and begins to stalk them, they know they must flee. Their harrowing journey takes them by oxen cart, train, and ship. Even within sight of America, their dream is threatened. Will all things work together for good in her life?

The second book, *GREEN as in Springtime, New Life, and God's Will* , begins in January of 1928, when the family arrives in Fond du Lac, Wisconsin. For twelve-year-old Lisenka and her family, Russia and persecution have been left far behind, but new problems face them. Lisenka must care for sick Taty, look after the little ones, and run the household. Even when she gets to go to school, she has obstacles because she's a German-speaking girl in a school that only teaches in English. Bullies make fun of her language and old-fashioned clothes, but with God's help and a few special friends, she perseveres. What is God's will for her in the springtime of her life?

WHITE as Christmas Snow, a Candle's Glow, and Heaven's Robe, set in December of 1929, continues Lisenka's story. The Great Depression is beginning to roll across America and so are men who are riding trains and looking for jobs. When fourteen-year-old Lisenka helps her friend Albert serve soup to men in a hobo jungle, she doesn't suspect that homelessness could soon threaten her own family. She learns the value of trusting God and being generous.

GOLD as October Sunsets, a Stray Dog, and God's Good Plans is the fourth book in the series. Set in October of 1930, the book focuses on almost fifteen-year-old Lisenka and her family as they reach out to young hobos, including one ten-year-old boy. The young hobos are afraid of being discovered and resist help. A stray golden retriever lopes onto the pages of the book and wins the hearts of Lisenka's family and the hobos, but the dog adds conflict too. Even in desperate times, Lisenka, her family, and friends learn that God does have a good plan for their lives.

All four Lisenka books are based on stories from actual people, real incidents, and the historical time but are works of fiction.

Historically, what was happening in 1930?

-Winnebago Lutheran Academy and St. Peter's Lutheran Church and School shared the same campus downtown, between First and Second streets. Today St. Peter's Place, apartments for seniors and office space, uses parts of the old buildings.

-Infant Socks Inc., located at 235 Superior Street, locally referred to as Five Points, began operations in Fond du Lac in 1929. It employed many young women in the knitting and shipping departments and a few men in maintenance and management. Today the area is a vacant lot.

-During the Great Depression, several hobo jungles sprang up in Fond du Lac, including two near Brooke Street, one on the north side of town, and one near the train yard in North Fond du Lac.

-During this period, many hobos passed through town, looking for work. Occasionally, a boy hobo might have appeared. Sometimes these boys had run away from an abusive home, and sometimes, if parents couldn't take care of all their children, boys were sent out on their own to earn their way.

-Infections were dangerous in 1930 because there was no antibiotic or penicillin. If infection set in, people could die of a simple cut or even a sliver.

-Automobiles did not have seat belts, so children often stood between the seats. Women rarely drove automobiles because it wasn't acceptable.

-Even in hard times, people liked to have fun. During parties, someone might bring out a stumpf fiddle, a homemade percussion instrument with bells, clangs, and noisemakers.

CHAPTER 1

October 1930
Fond du Lac, Wisconsin
Wednesday

"For I know the plans I have for you," declares the LORD, "plans to give you peace, not disaster, plans to give you hope and a future" (Jeremiah 29:11 EHV).

"Lis, watch me!" Seven-year-old Yurgi's voice echoed through the open kitchen window. I stood on tiptoe and peeked out. As soon as he saw me, he waved and threw a stick, then raced across the yard, sliding to a stop. He grabbed the stick and tumbled around in the leaves, laughing.

"What are you doing?" I shouted.

"I'm playing with my dog, Blackie." Yurgi rolled over and grinned at me. Crunchy leaves peppered his blonde hair and clung to his blue wool coat. I sighed, knowing his coat would have to be brushed off. And his head would need a good brushing too.

I yelled out the window again. "Quit making up stories! We don't have a dog. I already asked Papa, and he won't allow it. He says we don't even have enough food to feed us."

"I know." Yurgi's mouth turned down in a pout. "But my pretend dog won't eat much." He grabbed his pretend Blackie in a big hug.

I shook my head and turned back to cooking supper. As I dipped flour from the big bin in the cupboard and filled a bowl, I hummed to myself. Life was good for us, despite the Depression. Many men had lost their jobs. Banks were closing. People were living with less money or no money. But we had a house and enough simple food. Three years ago in Russia, I couldn't have imagined such a wonderful life.

I glanced at the note Taty and Papa had left on the table. It only said they would be home in time for supper. When they arrived, Papa would inhale and say, "What's that delicious smell, Lis?"

My stepmama Taty would give me a hug and say, "I can always count on you, Lisenka. You make the best dumplings."

The chicken broth on the stove steamed as I beat eggs and milk into the flour. The setting sun had turned our kitchen to a golden glow.

"Lisenka! Lis! He-e-e-l-p me!" Shrill screams shattered my peace.

My heart stopped, then it pounded in my chest. Yurgi! I froze, like my feet were stuck to the linoleum floor.

Alya, who had been studying her fourth-grade reader in the living room, charged into the kitchen, her eyes big. "What's wrong with Yurgi?"

I blinked, took a deep breath, and grabbed Alya's hand. We raced down the back steps and out the door. I caught a glimpse of a blue coat rolling on the ground beyond the chicken coop. Dusk was settling, so I squinted toward the tumbling blue. It was replaced by a rusty brown, then blue, then brown, tumbling over each other.

Yurgi was wrestling something, and it wasn't a pretend dog. Blue was on top now.

"Yurgi, what are you doing?" I tore across the yard.

"Lis, help me!" Yurgi gasped for breath, straddling a boy. "He was trying to take my favorite chicken, Rosie. That's stealing." Yurgi huffed for breath.

The boy clung to one of Rosie's legs. She squawked, flapped her wings, and pecked his hand, but he held on.

"We need this chicken." The boy yelled, kicked, and squirmed. "We need it more than you."

"You can't have Rosie." Yurgi stretched to grab the boy's hand, but he was bigger than Yurgi, wiggled free, and rolled over.

I was close enough to catch the boy by his shirt and pull him back. "What are you doing, you little thief?" I shouted.

Alya and Yurgi stood on both sides of me, staring the boy down. Three to one. We had him nabbed.

The boy, on his hands and knees, twisted around to glare at us. His brown eyes were set into a hollow, dirt-streaked face. His lips quivered. "Please, ma'am, we have to eat."

I swallowed a lump in my throat and loosened my grip on his tattered shirt for only a second. He scrambled up and sprinted off.

"Thanks, lady," he yelled over his shoulder, still holding Rosie's leg.

"Oh, no, you don't. We need to eat too." I dashed after him.

"Run, Lis!" Yurgi shouted.

"Hurry!" Alya yelled.

The boy cut around a bush beyond our yard. I charged after him, closing the gap. As my hand touched the bottom of his shirt, someone grabbed me around my waist and stopped me mid stride. A gruff voice whispered in my ear. "Let the boy go. I'll get your chicken."

I twisted around to see a grimy young man glaring at me. His tattered gray stocking cap shaded his dark eyes.

"We are not thieves, young lady, just hungry." He released his grip on me and stared at the boy scampering into the darkness. "Jimmy, get back here. Right now."

The boy stomped out of the shadows. "Ah, c'mon, Marty. They have a coop full of chickens."

Marty shook his head and pointed to the ground at my feet. "Here. Now."

Jimmy shuffled to where Marty pointed and dropped Rosie at my feet. Panting, Yurgi and Alya rushed up. Yurgi squatted beside Rosie, petting her, and she calmed down. Alya patted my back, and I calmed down. When I looked up, Jimmy and Marty were gone.

CHAPTER 2

That evening at supper, Yurgi told his story. "I tackled the chicken thief." Yurgi swallowed a bite of dumpling, his flushed face beaming. "He got away, but Lis stopped him."

Yurgi glanced sideways at me. "Well, almost stopped him. If we had a real dog, Blackie would have stopped him."

Papa raised one eyebrow. "We're not getting a dog, Yurgi. Now forget it. We can't afford to feed another mouth."

I frowned at Yurgi. "Let's tell the real story without the pretend Blackie." I turned to Papa. "Yurgi had already tackled the boy. He was maybe ten years old. I just grabbed his shirt to keep him from running."

Papa and Taty smiled at us across the kitchen table.

"This is a real good story the three of you hatched," Papa said.

"Hatched?" I laughed at Papa's chicken joke.

Papa nudged my foot under the table. I loved his little word jokes. He loved that I understood them.

Alya touched Papa's sleeve. "It's true. Lis had him until Marty grabbed Lis."

Papa gasped. "A man grabbed Lis?" He studied my face. "Did he hurt you?"

"No, Papa, it wasn't like that. I was protecting Yurgi, and Marty was protecting Jimmy."

"Who's Jimmy?"

Yurgi gulped down another bite without chewing. He tapped the table with exaggerated patience. "He is the chicken thief. Marty made Jimmy give Rosie back. Then poof, they disappeared."

Papa leaned back on his chair and chuckled. Taty's gentle laughter joined his as she scooted her chair back. "Thanks for cooking a delicious dumpling supper, Lisenka, and thanks to all of you for that entertaining story."

Papa stood too. "Taty and I have a few things to discuss, so we'll head into the living room while you clean up the kitchen and plan your next story." His laughter followed him from the kitchen.

"They don't believe us." Yurgi scowled.

"Probably because you added 'poof' to your story. 'Poof, they disappeared.' Why would Papa and Taty believe that?" I asked.

Yurgi plopped himself back on his chair and folded his arms. I let him pout.

Alya put the dishes into a tub and scraped a little soap over the top. I poured hot water from the kettle into the tub and scrubbed the dishes in the soapy water. Alya dried each dish as I handed it to her.

When the last dish was stacked on the table, I turned to Yurgi. "You have to put them away."

He crossed his arms tighter and stuck his chin up, staring out the darkened window.

"Yurgi, I mean it. You have to help too. Papa said." I planted my hands on my hips and scowled at Yurgi.

His eyes got big, and he screamed. "Jimmy! I saw him peeking in our window."

When I twirled around, I only saw a dark window. Papa and Taty rushed into the kitchen. "What's wrong?" Papa asked.

Yurgi's face was pale. "P-p-papa, somebody was peeking in our window. I think it was Jimmy."

"Nobody should be peeking in our windows." Papa dashed down the back steps two at a time.

The rest of us clambered behind and caught up with Papa outside the kitchen window. Nobody was there.

Yurgi's mouth hung open. "Poof!" he whispered.

Papa glanced from Yurgi to the window then to me.

"How tall was Jimmy?"

"Hmm." I frowned, picturing him. "Shorter than me. Taller than Alya. Probably less than five feet tall, but he was skinny."

Papa pointed to the window. "Well, he couldn't have been peeking in this window without help. It's six feet off the ground." He squatted and pointed to the grass. "But see how the grass is stomped down? Somebody was definitely here."

We crowded around. The light from the window helped us see faint footprints.

I pointed to the loose dirt against the house. "Look here. I can see big and smaller footprints."

Papa tipped back on his heels. "That means a bigger person probably lifted the little person up to spy on us."

"Well, children." Taty pushed us toward the back door. "Your story is starting to make sense. But why are strangers lurking outside our house?" She shivered. "Let's get inside and lock the door."

I tugged on Taty's sleeve. "Maybe it's Marty and Jimmy again. I wonder who they are."

Papa joined us by the door. Holding it open, he peered into the darkness. "Could they be living in the hobo jungle?"

Since the Depression started last year, more men were forced to leave home to find jobs. They often lived in out-of-the-way vacant lots. We called their camps hobo jungles. During the winter, we had taken food to the hobos but hadn't visited during the summer. We never went to the hobo jungle alone. It could be a dangerous place.

I strained to see through the darkness too. "But Jimmy is a little boy, Papa. He couldn't be a hobo, could he?"

CHAPTER 3

Thursday

The next morning, Yurgi stood watch at the living room window. "Max and Hildy are here," he yelled.

I finished brushing Alya's blonde hair and tied it with a blue ribbon.

"That's the perfect color for you." I stepped back to admire. "The ribbon matches your eyes."

Alya blushed and darted from our bedroom, the room that we three children shared.

I fluffed my short brown hair with my fingers and hurried behind her out the front door. "Aren't you a little early, Max?"

"One can never be too prompt in arriving at school, especially high school, especially Winnebago Lutheran Academy," Max said in a deep voice.

Hildy, his twin sister, giggled. "Really, Max. We all know that your voice is changing, but do you have to make it so low and proper?"

"That's my regular voice, Hildy." Max strutted to her and glared down. At age fourteen, he was taller than his sister, but their red, unruly hair still matched. Their little arguments continued too.

"Well." I stepped between them. "Let's get going." I called toward the kitchen door. "Taty, we're leaving."

She hurried in, drying her hands on her apron. "Goodbye, children. Have a blessed day. Be a blessing."

"Bye, Mama." Alya and Yurgi waved as they jumped down the stairs.

"Bye, Taty." I flashed a grin at my stepmother. Soon it would be her and Papa's tenth wedding anniversary. I would need to do something to celebrate the day she filled the emptiness left in my heart when Mama died.

"I'll be working at Mrs. Wilson's house after school," she said. "Please help the little ones with their homework and peel some potatoes. I'm bringing a ham home." She paused. A flicker of fear crossed her face. "Do you have your key? I'll have the house locked up."

I pulled the key, tied in a handkerchief, from my pocket and held it up.

"Good." Taty nodded. "Lock the doors."

Lock the doors.

I hurried to catch up with the others as *lock the doors* echoed in my head. Should we be that worried about a little boy and a young man, maybe only a teenager? What harm could they do?

Yurgi twisted backward and flapped his hand at me. "Hurry up, Lisenka. We were telling Max and Hildy about last night. Tell them I really did tackle Jimmy."

I raised my eyebrows and nodded.

"Stealing chickens is a serious offense." Max paused. "We should report this to the police."

"Really, Max? The police?" Hildy shook her head. "One little boy took one chicken and returned it."

"I'm just saying that a crime was committed."

We had a lively conversation every weekday as the five of us walked the mile to St. Peter's Lutheran School and Winnebago Lutheran Academy on Second Street. The buildings were next to each other. Today's conversation was livelier than normal.

Yurgi jumped in front of Max. "I could have been hurt. What if Jimmy broke my arm or gave me a black eye?"

"Yurgi, none of that happened." I grabbed him by his shoulders. "We're not going to tell the police that something could have happened."

Max turned Yurgi to face him. "I'm with you, little buddy. We've got a problem here."

Yurgi stood taller. Any day he could impress Max was a good day.

A frown puckered Alya's face. I grabbed her hand and tugged her along. "Don't worry, Alya. We will be fine. For now, we better keep moving."

I glanced at Max. "We want to be prompt arriving at school, like you said." I lowered my voice slightly.

"Oh, right." Max didn't notice my joke.

He grabbed Yurgi's hand and pulled him along. I kept a firm hold on Alya and linked arms with Hildy as we turned onto Main Street. Officer Kowalski, dressed in a black uniform, was on the next corner, strolling toward us, doing his morning beat through downtown. He stopped to jiggle locked doors, making sure they were secure, and tipped his black-billed hat to a lady on the corner.

My back stiffened as he approached us. Even though we had been in America almost three years now, men in uniforms still sent a quiver of fear down my spine. In Russia, soldiers hurt us German-Russian people. They closed our school and chopped up our desks. They forbid us to worship God. They starved us. And the worst one, Commandant Chukov, almost captured us when we escaped

The little ones had no memories of the terrors we suffered in Russia, but I could not forget. I took a deep breath as Officer Kowalski strolled toward us, his black shiny boots reflecting the sunlight. My knees quivered as I stared at the gun and billy club hanging from his belt, but I still gave him a guarded smile. Yurgi broke free from Max's grasp and ran to him.

"Officer Kowalski, you have to help us." Yurgi tugged on the officer's coat. "Marty and Jimmy are stealing our chickens."

Officer Kowalski knelt to face Yurgi. "Oh, no! What can you tell me about these thieves?"

CHAPTER 4

Officer Kowalski asked us many more questions and made notes in his little book. Max pulled out his pocket watch and frowned. I glanced at the time over his shoulder. A prompt arrival at school was impossible now. In fact, we'd all be getting tardy slips.

"That will be all for now." Officer Kowalski tucked his little book into his coat pocket. "I have your home address, so I'll stop in later to talk to your parents." He turned to continue walking his route.

"Thank you, officer." I pasted a smile on my face and grabbed hold of Yurgi's arm, yanking him down the street. "Didn't I tell you to forget it?" I hissed and gave his arm another yank.

"Lis, you're hurting me." He whimpered, his big blue eyes filling with tears. "Max thought we should tell." I released my grip and patted Yurgi's arm.

"Really, Max?" Hildy bit her lip. "You're telling one little boy to tattle on another?"

"We need to nip crime immediately." Max shrugged and marched ahead. There was no happy chatter the rest of the way, only silence. We turned onto Second Street as the tardy bell rang. Yurgi and Alya raced up the steps of St. Peter's.

The rest of us ran a few more steps. A shiny beige Model A Ford was parked by the steps of the academy. As we got closer, the sound of its motor purring reached my ears. Eddy Monroe stepped from the car. His long legs carried him around it, and his six-foot tall body blocked the sidewalk. He crossed his arms.

"Oh, no." My shoulders slumped. How could Eddy Monroe show up on the only day we'd been late this semester?

Max and Hildy stood on each side of me. A two-person support team.

"Lis, I'm surprised that you're not more diligent in getting to school, especially since I'm paying your way."

Max came to my defense, using his most manly voice. "Mr. Monroe, we are always prompt. I make sure of it, but today we have a good excuse."

Eddy raised an eyebrow at Max and pointed to the door. "I'm not interested in your excuses. You two better scurry inside. This is between Lis and me."

Max and Hildy squirmed and ran up the steps. My support team was gone. I squirmed, too, but held my ground. Eddy and I had formed a bit of a friendship after his elderly mother died. I had worked for her, for them really, during her final months. She knew my dream was to finish eighth grade, but I had to help our family pay the bills. Before Mrs. Monroe died of a stroke, she put money aside for my family so I could go to school. Her kind gesture surprised all of us, even her 50-year-old son Eddy.

Sometimes she confided in me, saying, "Eddy is a nice boy, but he's spoiled and selfish." Then she would say, "Don't tell Eddy I said that."

I smiled at the memory. Eddy put his face down to mine. "Something funny here?"

I stumbled back a step. "No, Eddy, I was just remembering your sweet mother. I'm glad I got to know her. And I'm glad you and I have become friends."

"Friends don't use friends unjustly." Eddy took a step forward. "I stopped at school to make another payment on your tuition, and I find you dawdling down the sidewalk."

"Eddy, we were stopped by a policeman because somebody tried to steal a chicken last night."

"What?"

"It's a long story, and you really have to hear it from Yurgi." I put my hand over my mouth to hide a smile, picturing poor Eddy cornered by Yurgi and his expanding story.

"Your friendship and your assistance mean more to me than you can ever imagine," I continued. "I've been a diligent student. Just ask my teachers. Getting an education has been my lifelong dream. I'd be scrubbing floors and mending shirts if it weren't for you."

Eddy whistled softly and blinked. "I'm sorry. I get riled up too easily. I'm sure my mother told you that too." He grinned. "And I'm sure my mother would be thrilled that I'm able to send you to the academy."

Someone shouted from behind me, and I spun around. Miss Meuschlin, Yurgi's teacher, hurried down the sidewalk, waving her handkerchief. Strands of her dark brown hair framed her face. She had been my teacher when we first arrived in Fond du Lac. She'd helped me through my struggles and had become my friend.

Now she stood panting in front of us. "Mr. Monroe, I'm so glad I caught you. Is everything alright? Yurgi told me you were outside with Lis."

"Yes, all is well." Eddy beamed at Miss Meuschlin. She blushed. I cleared my throat to get their attention, but they didn't notice.

CHAPTER 5

As we walked home from school, Albert slid up beside me. Albert was my first friend in America, a special friend. He had helped us adjust to life in America and I loved him like a brother, maybe a little more. But sometimes he irritated me like a brother.

"What were you doing talking to a policeman this morning?" Albert stepped in front of me.

"How do you know that?" I lifted my chin and scooted around him. "Do you think you need to know everything that happens in Fond du Lac?"

"I have my contacts. Plus, I'm just naturally curious." He trotted beside me.

"You mean nosy?" I covered my mouth to hide a grin.

Albert's brown eyes twinkled. He liked when I teased him. Even though Albert was only seventeen, he had quit school a couple of years earlier to help his family pay the bills. First he worked by delivering items for a hardware store, then he started his own delivery business.

Max squeezed between Albert and me. "We were reporting an attempted robbery."

"A robbery?" Albert gasped. "Where?"

"Let me tell you about it." Yurgi grabbed Albert's hand and tugged him to a halt.

The rest of us kept going. I called over my shoulder, "Please bring Yurgi home. His story might take a while." I glimpsed Albert's downturned mouth, and I added, "Plan to stay for supper."

+ + + + +

The five of us, plus Albert, sat around our kitchen table, heads bowed, hands folded, as Papa prayed. "Dear Lord, thank You for the many blessings You've showered on us in America, blessings like good friends, Christian schools, a Gospel-preaching church, a warm house, and a delicious ham for tonight's supper. We praise You because all good gifts come from You. In Jesus' name. Amen."

Taty and Papa filled our plates with boiled potatoes, applesauce, and tiny pieces of ham. Then they settled into their chairs.

Yurgi jumped up. "I have another story for you, Papa and Mama."

Papa shook his head, and Yurgi sank into his chair.

"Before your story, Yurgi, Taty and I have some exciting news to share. Go ahead, Taty. You go first."

Taty's cheeks glowed as she sat up straighter. "I have a real job. On Monday, I'll start work at the Infant Socks Factory, just a few blocks away at Five Points."

Nobody moved, just stared at Taty, puzzled. Taty wasn't supposed to work except for a few hours here and there at Mrs. Wilson's house. Taty was tender, still recovering from tuberculosis. We needed to take care of her. What was she thinking? I swallowed the bite of potato that I'd forgotten to chew and coughed.

Taty glanced around the table. "Infant Socks has only been in Fond du Lac for a year and already it is one of the biggest sock factories in the country. Even now, during the Depression, they are hiring. Three hundred women work there doing knitting, sewing, and bundling. Mrs. Wilson recommended me because of my sewing skills. Can you believe I'll make fifty cents a day?" A flush lit her face.

We were silent.

"Isn't that good news?" Papa took Taty's hand, waiting for us to answer.

"That is good news." I tried to smile. "Will you work every day?"

"Ja, every day, 6 a.m. to 1 p.m., but not Sundays. The second shift of women works longer hours, from 1 to 10 p.m. But I like this schedule because I can be home evenings."

"What about mornings?" Alya asked. "Who will get us up for school?"

"Who will pack my lunch?" Yurgi frowned. "You always know how much peanut butter to put on my bread."

"Don't worry, Taty." I reached for the little ones' hands. "We can take care of the morning chores. We'll work together. The extra money you earn will help us, right?"

Papa rested his arms on the table. "Now for my news."

I wasn't sure I wanted more news, but Papa continued. "As you know, I've gone to Nebraska twice to help with the sugar beet crops. In December I worked in the processing factories, and this spring I returned for the planting."

"Oh, no, Papa." I grabbed his sleeve. "You can't go away again."

Papa patted my hand. "The pay is good in Nebraska, and they offered me a job this fall. I stalled, trying to decide. Then I heard that Infant Socks needed a maintenance man, so I applied there."

I held my breath. Alya and Yurgi stared at Papa, tears brimming.

Papa paused and raised his arms. "I got the job. I'm staying in Fond du Lac. I can go to work with Taty every day."

I jumped up so fast my chair clattered over. "Wahoo!" The little ones joined me in dancing around the table. Albert grinned at our antics.

After we settled down, Yurgi took a deep breath. "Now it's time for my story.

Papa and Taty, you will be happy to know that Max and I reported the thief."

Papa's fork clattered to the floor. "You what?"

A knock sounded on the front door. Yurgi interrupted his story to race to the door.

"It's Officer Kowalski," he yelled. In a moment, the officer strolled into the kitchen, dragging a dirty young man in handcuffs. Yurgi trailed behind.

"I got your thief. Well, at least, his accomplice. This here lad is Marty."

The young man was almost six feet tall. His dark straight hair hung in greasy swirls. Crusty dirt coated his face. He scowled at me. I scowled back and shook my head.

"That's not Marty."

CHAPTER 6

"This is not Marty?" Officer Kowalski stepped in front of the man and yelled in his face. "You told me your name was Marty."

The young man cringed and stared at the floor.

Taty cringed, too, and reached for Alya, hugging her and pulling her against the far wall. She squeezed her eyes shut, trembling. Albert edged toward Taty and put a kind arm around her and Alya.

Papa leaped up, cocking his head sideways. "What is going on here?"

"I was trying to tell you," Yurgi said.

"Well, start telling." Papa clipped his words.

Yurgi took a deep breath to start telling, but more loud pounding came from the front door, and it slammed open. Again, Yurgi ran to see. "It's Heinrich," he yelled. "And..."

Heinrich burst into the kitchen. Heinrich was like an uncle to us, so he usually didn't wait for us to answer the door, but he usually didn't roar into the kitchen either. He and his wife Rachel were loving friends to our family.

"I found these two scoundrels lurking outside your house, peeking in the side window." He held each one's jacket in a tight grip and thrust them forward.

I gasped and pointed to the bigger boy, still several inches shorter than the pretend Marty. His ratty gray stocking hat and dark eyes were the same. "That's Marty."

"And this is Jimmy, the chicken thief." Yurgi clenched his fists and marched up to the smaller one.

I yanked Yurgi back, and Papa swung him to his hip with a firm hand.

Heinrich screwed up his face. "You know these window peepers?"

"Well, well, well, what a happy little party we have here." Officer Kowalski narrowed his eyes and rubbed his jaw. "Now tell me. Who is the real Marty?"

The young man held in Heinrich's strong grip lifted one limp hand but kept his head down.

Officer Kowalski strutted over, tapping his billy club on his knee. "Whose idea was it to steal a chicken?"

Marty shifted his feet. His shoulders slumped. He answered with a gruff voice. "It was my idea. My brother Jimmy is small enough to slip through tiny places, like a chicken fence, so I sent him."

"That's not true," Jimmy sputtered, glaring at Marty. "It was my idea. Marty told me it was wrong, but I did it anyway. We're hungry, mister."

Officer Kowalski's face relaxed. He motioned for Heinrich to release his grip on the two and knelt in front of Jimmy. "How old are you, son? Where are your parents? Shouldn't they be taking care of you?"

Jimmy's chin shook, and his eyes filled with tears. "I'm ten. We don't have family no more." He crossed his arms and added, "And I'm glad."

Marty's voice quavered. "My brother and I are traveling to find cousins in Missouri, but we ran out of money. We've been riding the rails and living in hobo jungles until we get there."

Officer Kowalski took off his hat and rubbed his head. He studied Jimmy and rubbed his head some more. Then he plopped his hat back on, grabbed hold of the table, and heaved himself up. He faced the pretend Marty.

"So who are you?"

The pretend Marty hunched his shoulders and sighed. "My name is Roy. I'm sorry I lied to you, officer. I'm traveling along with my friends here, trying to protect them. When I heard you were going to arrest Marty, I pretended to be him." Roy glanced at Marty. His head hung forward. "I can handle jail better than he can."

"Well, I never heard anything like this." Officer Kowalski tugged his little book from his pocket and began to read. "Let's see what we have here. First, Jimmy and Marty attempted to steal a chicken but returned it when they were tackled by Lis, Alya, and Yurgi."

Yurgi grinned at Alya and me. We grinned back.

"Next, we think Jimmy was peeking in the window last night, probably assisted by Marty, but this is unproven," Officer Kowalski said. "And now we have Roy's recent crime of lying to a police officer."

Officer Kowalski turned to Papa. "Mr. Schallert, would you like to press charges against any of these people for any of their crimes?"

Papa rubbed his forehead.

Taty stepped forward, tears brimming in her eyes. "Pavel, they're poor, hungry children. We can't send them to jail for trying to keep from starving. Our cupboard is still filled with bowls of potatoes, ham, and applesauce. Please, let's feed them and let them go."

Papa nodded. Every person in the room sighed with relief. While Officer Kowalski unlocked the handcuffs on Roy, I took three plates from the cupboard and filled them with food.

"Please sit and eat," Taty said.

With sparkling eyes, the three scooted into chairs and shoveled in the food.

Officer Kowalski watched the happy scene for a few minutes. "Well, I wish all crime scenes ended so well." He shook Papa's hand and headed for the front door.

Heinrich followed. "Albert, do you need a ride home? I'll be driving by your place."

"I sure appreciate the offer." Albert chuckled. "I'm exhausted from all the excitement. Who would guess that a simple supper invitation would turn into a crime scene?" Albert nudged me with his elbow. I nudged him back.

"Yep, no end to the craziness of this household." Heinrich thumped Papa on the back and laughed as they headed for the front door.

The rest of us followed the friendly banter into the living room, but when I heard a rustling noise behind me, I turned. The backdoor slammed shut and the chairs around the table were empty.

CHAPTER 7

"They're gone." I dashed through the kitchen and down the steps to the backdoor, flung it open, and peered into the darkness. Nothing.

Yurgi clomped down the steps behind me. "Can you see them? How could they disappear again?"

We squinted into the night. I cupped my hands and shouted. "Jimmy! Marty! Roy! Come back. We can help you. Don't hide again."

Papa raced past us and circled the chicken pen. In a few minutes, he returned, scratching his head. "Nothing."

"Poof," whispered Yurgi.

Taty and Alya stood on the top step, arms around each other. "Come back in," Taty said. "We can't do anything more tonight."

With heavy feet, we filed into the kitchen. I was exhausted from the excitement too. "We need some hot tea." I filled the kettle with water and put it on the stove to heat. While I sprinkled dried tea leaves into the kettle, Taty and Papa collapsed onto two chairs at the table. Alya pushed her chair against Taty's.

Papa pulled Yurgi onto his lap. "Maybe it's time to hear the rest of your story."

Yurgi leaned back with a yawn. "There's not much more to tell."

Papa gave him a hug. "I want to hear about Officer Kowalski."

Yurgi sat tall and finished his story while Papa listened. His lips lifted in a half smile.

I poured the tea through a strainer into five cups and set them on the table. Papa was still smiling as Yurgi snored.

I curled my lips. "Why would Yurgi have to tattle on a little boy? I told him to forget it, then Max told him it was the right thing. But it wasn't. Look at all the trouble it brought us."

Papa studied my face, his lips set in a tight, straight line. I rubbed my hands on my apron, avoiding his practicing patience look.

"Maybe it was the right thing," he said. "Marty and Jimmy were stealing our property and spying on us. Is that right?"

I blew on my hot tea and watched it swirl.

Papa rested his hand on mine. "Getting caught might have actually saved them."

I pulled my hand back. "From what?"

"From stealing bigger things, from going to jail, maybe even from a life of crime. What does the Seventh Commandment say, Lis?"

I stared at the ceiling, trying to remember. Alya piped in, "Thou shalt not steal." She leaned forward. "What does this mean? We should fear and love God so that we do not take our neighbor's money or property or get it by dishonest dealings, but help him to improve and protect his property and business."

Taty patted Alya's leg. "I didn't know you could recite the Seventh Commandment."

Alya lifted her chin. "I know all ten."

Papa's mouth hung open. "What a wonderful thing. Our children are learning the Ten Commandments. We are blessed."

Taty glanced at Papa. Her eyes twinkled.

I hoped he was done lecturing me, but he swiveled in his chair to face me head on. "Does the Seventh Commandment say you should not steal unless you're hungry or unless you're ten years old?"

"No."

"Does it say we should look the other way if we catch someone stealing?"

"No."

"Should I have pressed charges?"

"No."

"Really? Why?"

I frowned, thinking. "Because maybe they learned their lesson just by getting caught and maybe because they are hungry and young. There might be a better way to teach them."

"That's exactly what I was thinking." Papa took a sip of tea. "Do you know the Golden Rule? It's what Jesus says in Matthew 7:12."

I shook my head. So did Alya. Papa continued, "'Do for others whatever you want people to do for you.' Let's see if we can treat them how we'd like to be treated. But first we have to find them."

I snapped my fingers. "I have a nosy friend who can sniff them out."

Papa chuckled. He understood my word joke.

CHAPTER 8

Friday

The next day as we walked home from school, Yurgi and Alya chased each other in circles, laughing and kicking leaves.

"What are you doing tomorrow?" Max sidestepped Yurgi and then thrust his shoulders back. "I plan to spend the day writing my research paper."

"Really, Max?" Hildy twirled to face him. "You're going to waste a beautiful fall Saturday inside Grandma's house, studying books. Saturdays are for fun."

"Studying is fun."

"No, it's work."

"I think it's fun."

"Well, I don't."

Albert ran up behind us, sliding to a halt beside me. I pressed my hands to my eyes. "Thanks for arriving at this moment. The twins are arguing again."

"We were not!" Max said.

"You were. I wasn't." Hildy blew out a big breath.

"Stop!" I clamped my hands over my ears, glaring at both of them.

They stopped. I took my hands from my ears but held up a warning finger. No more arguing erupted.

I turned to Albert. "You are just the person I wanted to see."

"I am?" He flashed a big smile. "Usually, you have a smart comment for me and keep walking."

"Yea." Max elbowed his way between us. "Why do you want to see him when you're walking with me?"

I patted Max's arm. "You're the smartest boy I know when it comes to book learning." Max gave me a knowing nod. "But

Albert has street smarts, and he's naturally curious, as he likes to say. I need his talents today for a secret job."

Max's shoulders sagged. "C'mon, Hildy, we're not wanted here. Let's keep going to Grandma's house." He stomped down the sidewalk.

I grabbed Hildy's hand. "Could you take Alya and Yurgi along?"

"Sure. Grandma will love to see them and will probably have warm cookies waiting for us."

"Thank you, Lis!" The little ones pranced in front of me.

"I'll pick you up later. Be sure to thank Frau Brunhild and only eat one cookie."

Yurgi stared up with big eyes. "Really?"

"Well, maybe two."

"Wahoo! Wait for me." Yurgi skipped after them.

We watched them get a block ahead and then Albert lifted one eyebrow. "What's my secret job?" he whispered.

I linked arms with him and tugged him along. "It's not that secret, but I didn't want the others to hear. Can you help me check out the hobo jungle behind our house? Last night, as you walked out the front door, Marty, Jimmy, and Roy escaped out the backdoor."

Albert blew out a breath. "You think I'll find them in the hobo jungle?"

"Maybe. They were camping there."

"I love snooping around. Thanks for sending me."

"I'm not sending you. I want you to come with me."

Albert's face lit up. "I love adventures with you even more. Let's go get your disguise."

CHAPTER 9

At home, Albert waited in the living room while I dashed into my bedroom to change clothes.

When I strolled out a few minutes later, Albert whistled. "You look as good as ever. Who would guess that you're a girl dressed in Eddy's old brown trousers and coat?"

I turned around for his inspection.

"Wait," he said. "Your hair is hanging out the back of your newsboy hat."

I whipped the hat off, stooped over so my short brown hair hung down, and tucked it into my hat again.

Albert checked. "That's good. Let's go. Remember, I'm doing all the talking. You sound too much like a girl."

I frowned up at him. "Thank you, I think."

He chuckled and held the front door open. We hurried past a few houses on Brooke Street and turned down a dirt road.

Where it dead ended by the river, the hobo jungle began. We stopped and scanned the area.

Last winter, Albert and I brought a kettle of soup to the hobos on Monday afternoons, but when the weather warmed in the spring, he didn't think it was necessary. The place hadn't changed much. Cardboard boxes, used as shelters, were strewn around. Some leaned against tangled trees. Others were propped on barrels. A few rough-looking men, dressed in tattered clothes, squatted by a small fire. Some twisted around to stare. A hobo pushed himself up and sauntered over. One sleeve was ripped on his black-and-green plaid jacket. Several buttons were missing. He stopped a few feet from us, planted his saggy boots two feet apart, and snarled, "Whatcha boys want?"

My knees shook. I shoved my hands in my pockets and quit breathing for a second.

But Albert was calm. "Hello, sir. We're looking for three runaways. One is a boy about ten. The other two are in their teens. Have you seen them?"

He chewed on his bottom lip. "They're not here."

Albert's smile faded. "Please, sir, we want to help them. The little one is half starved."

The hobo rubbed his crusty eyes. Pity filled his face when he looked up. "Yeah, I saw them. What a shame for parents to send a boy out to fend for himself, even if the other two are trying to help. Yeah, they were here."

The man frowned. "Last evening, about dusk, a policeman showed up, said he was looking for Marty. The rest of us scattered, even the younger two, but the biggest boy strutted right up to that policeman. 'I'm Marty,' he said."

The hobo swept his hand toward the river. "I was peeking from behind that yonder bush. I couldn't believe my eyes. The policemen whipped out his handcuffs and cuffed the poor boy right on the spot, then dragged him up the road to who knows where."

To our house. And now they were running again, far away from where we could help them. I blinked back tears. A heavy weight settled on my chest.

But Albert hadn't given up. He smiled at the man. "It's getting chilly out. Winter might not be far away. Please spread the word to your friends that Albert's soup kettle is back. I'll be delivering hot soup here tomorrow at noon. And every Saturday thereafter."

The hobo's face broke into a big grin. He was missing several teeth, but his smile was still beautiful. "I will let everyone know, son. Thank you kindly."

Albert and I hurried back to Brooke Street before talking. "How was that for being street smart?" Albert clapped his hands.

I tucked a stray strand of hair under my hat and frowned at Albert. "You were smart, but how does bringing a kettle of soup to a hobo jungle make you street smart?"

Albert took a slight bow. "Simple, my dear. It's the law of the street. If free food is being served, word will spread, even to other hobo jungles."

"Ah." I nodded. "If Marty, Jimmy, and Roy are in town, they'll be here tomorrow at noon."

CHAPTER 10

Saturday

Albert hoisted a big kettle of chicken vegetable soup onto our stovetop to warm. He'd pulled it in his wagon from home. Then he turned to my whole family, gathered in the kitchen. "Doesn't Albert's Soup Saturday have a nice ring to it? I like it better than Soup Monday, don't you?"

Papa slapped him on the back and laughed. "Ja, but what's even better is your kindness. Many of these men would love a warm house, a good job, and a cup of hot soup. How nice that you can give them the soup."

Albert blushed. Papa's praise did that to him.

I fidgeted with my hat. "Taty, is all my hair tucked in?"

She twirled me around. "You're ready."

"The soup is steaming." Albert took hold of the kettle handle with a dish towel, and I took the tray of cups Alya had stacked.

Yurgi stomped his foot. "I should be allowed to come along. I know Jimmy. We're almost friends."

Papa scooped up Yurgi. "Jimmy will run away from you because you tattled on him. They'd probably run away from all of us. That's why Lis is in disguise. I don't think they'll know her. And I doubt they'll recognize Albert since they barely saw him." Papa studied Albert, pulled his coat collar up and his hat down. "There."

"Be careful," Taty called from the front door where they stood, watching as we started down the street. "Don't say anything to the men."

I blew a kiss to Taty and made a zipping motion across my mouth. Everyone laughed as Papa nudged them back inside. The sun was shining, but frost had nipped the flowers overnight.

I tugged at my hat. "What will we do or say if we find them? We can't tackle them again, but we can't let them run away again either."

"I've been thinking about that too. If they show up, let's not say anything. We can listen to any conversation they might have with each other. A hint about where they're from or where they're going could be helpful. And we can watch which direction they go after they eat."

"Good idea."

As we neared the hobo jungle, we saw many more men milling around today. I tried to not smile. The word about Albert's Soup Saturday had indeed spread.

Albert balanced the kettle on a flat stump and called out. "Welcome to Albert's Soup Saturday. If you'd like a cup of hot chicken vegetable soup, please line up."

I stood beside Albert, balancing the tray on my shaking hands. I kept my head low, but my eyes were busy, checking out every corner of the hobo jungle. No boy or teenager was in sight.

Albert picked up one cup from my tray for a dipper and began to fill another. "Come one, come all." He smiled at the first hobo who grabbed a cupful of soup. "Thanks to Bart the butcher for giving me some scrap chicken bones, and thanks to George the grocer for providing the vegetables. Oh, and thanks to me, Albert, for putting it all together."

"Aren't you going to thank the poor boy holding the heavy tray?" the man in the black-and-green jacket asked.

"Of course." Albert rolled his hand and bowed. "Most importantly of all, thanks to my buddy, L-L-Lester, for holding the heavy tray."

Albert nudged me with his elbow. I glared back. He almost ruined my disguise.

But the men didn't seem to notice. Instead, they chuckled at Albert's antics and stood around in a circle, slurping up the fragrant soup. A few more sauntered over from the trees near the river, and Albert filled cups for them too.

He put his hand up, shading his eyes, and made an exaggerated show of peering one way and the other. "Anyone else?" Again the men chuckled and stacked their empty cups onto my tray.

The man in the black-and-green plaid jacket stepped forward. "Thank you for that delicious dinner. It's almost as good as my wife's cooking." He gazed into the distant trees and sighed, then shook his head. "Sorry the three runaways didn't show up. I reckon they're all the way to Madison by now."

CHAPTER 11

Yurgi flung the door open before we got to the steps. "Did you find my new friend, Jimmy?"

"Sorry, little man." Albert ruffled Yurgi's hair as we shuffled past him and into the kitchen. He put the kettle back on the hot stove. "Anyone want some chicken vegetable soup? We have enough left for a few more bowls. I'll warm it up."

Taty touched Albert's arm as he stirred the soup. "Did you catch a glimpse of the children?"

"Nothing."

Taty slumped into a chair, and I slouched in a chair next to hers. "Albert had such a smart plan. Why didn't it work?"

Taty rubbed the embroidered flower on her apron. "I wish we had been kinder to that little boy when he sat in this chair. I wish I had taken his hand and offered him a warm bed."

I patted Taty's hand. "We were as kind as we could be. Everything happened fast. We let them go free from Officer Kowalski. We fed them supper. How did we know they would still run away?"

"Poof." Yurgi crawled onto my lap. "I should have been a better friend. I should have given him Rosie." He sniffed into my shoulder.

I rubbed his back. Albert set a small bowl of steaming soup and a spoon in front of each of us. "Eat. You will feel better. Maybe food will help us think better. Do we have any clues?"

I sipped soup from my spoon and closed my eyes. I took another sip and one big clue popped into my head. "That man knew something, the one who talked to us yesterday and today. Remember what he said?"

Albert sat down beside me. "I do. He said what a shame it is for parents to send a boy out to fend for himself."

I bolted upright. "That means they have parents, but Jimmy said he had no family. That must have been a lie."

"Parents?" Taty chimed in. "What kind of parents would send a little boy off?"

Papa sat across the table, rubbing his chin. "How does Marty fit into the story? He said that Jimmy was his brother."

"An older boy, like Marty, could hold a job and help the family," Albert said. "Maybe there were many younger children, so

Jimmy was told to leave. There were too many mouths to feed and not enough money."

I tapped my spoon on the table. "What if Marty, the older brother, decided to come along with Jimmy, unknown to his parents. Of course, he loved his little brother and wanted to protect him."

I leaned back on my chair. "Oh, here's another clue. That man said they were probably to Madison by now. Why would he say Madison?"

Papa nodded. "But the boys did say they were traveling to Missouri to find some cousins. Madison is on the way."

"I can't make sense of it." Albert took another bite of soup, then he dropped his spoon. "But someone might be able to."

"Of course," I said.

And Albert continued my thought. "We have to talk to that old man again."

I stuffed my hair into my hat as Albert and I ran out the front door.

CHAPTER 12

At the edge of the hobo jungle, we stooped over, panting, catching our breath. Albert straightened up first. "Let's be careful. I feel safer here on the edge of the lot than down by the river in the trees."

I stood up, too, peering toward the edges of the hobo jungle. "Do you see him?" A few men leaned on trees, sat on rocks around the smoking fire, or huddled together talking, but many had disappeared. "Where is everyone?"

Albert scratched his head. "On Saturday afternoons, many homeless men get odd jobs around town, raking leaves or digging up the final vegetables in gardens. Some might be doing that."

We walked farther into the hobo jungle. I peeked into boxes and squinted toward the bushes and trees along the river, hoping to catch a glimpse of a black-and-green plaid jacket.

Albert grabbed my arm and turned me back. "That's far enough. We'll have to try again on another day."

My shoulders slumped. "In another day, poor Jimmy could be too weak to walk. Oh, why didn't they come for Soup Saturday?"

"Albert! Lester!" A voice called from somewhere.

I twirled around and grabbed Albert's arm. "Who yelled?" I whispered. "Where did that cry come from?"

"I'm over yonder. Here." Someone called from a grove of trees to our left, closer to Brooke Street but deep in the tangle of bushes.

I swung around in that direction, my breath catching in my throat. Albert raised his arm in front of me. "This could be a trap. We'd be all alone in there with a stranger. Nobody could see us from Brooke Street, and the hobos are farther back along the river. Who would even know if we got beaten up? I can't take you back there."

My knees got jittery, but I folded my hands and held them at my chest. "Please, Albert. We have to go. We just brought soup to these men. They won't repay a kind deed with evil, will they?"

Albert glanced from me to the dark grove of trees and back at me. He picked up a big stick, the size of a baseball bat, and tapped it in his hand. "Alright. Stay beside me, right beside me. Let's go."

As we crept closer, I spied a black-and-green plaid jacket and pointed. "There he is, in the shadow of that big tree.

The hobo sat propped against the tree, waving one arm. We hurried over. He grimaced and struggled to stand but slid back down.

"Excuse me, boys. I think I'll just stay seated to talk."

"Please, don't stand," Albert said. "What happened?"

"After you left, I thought about your search for the three boys. I decided to tell you what I know, but in my hurry, I stepped into a hole, and I twisted my ankle. It's just sprained, but it sure hurts to walk on it."

"Maybe we should take you to a doctor." Albert knelt down for a closer look. "It's already swelling."

The man flicked his hand. "Not necessary. I've been spraining this darn ole ankle my whole life. I'll just take it easy for a couple days."

I squatted beside Albert and asked in my gruff voice, "What else do you have to tell us? We tried to put some clues together, and they led us back to you."

"Well, I'm not rightly sure I can tell you much, but I do know a bit more." He pushed himself straighter and thrust out his hand to Albert. "Excuse my bad manners. My name is Austin. I already know you're Albert and L-L-Lester."

Albert stood and shook his hand. "I'm glad to meet you, Austin."

I reached out, too, but instead of a handshake, Austin held my hand and patted it with his left. "Small hand," he said. I yanked it away and stood up as a shiver of fear ran down my spine.

Albert cleared his throat, a frown pulling his eyebrows down. He stepped between me and the hobo. "Just tell us what you know."

Austin blinked his eyes. "Yeah, I'll tell you what I know. I've heard them talking to each other. Marty and Jimmy come from a big family. Marty is the oldest, followed by two sisters, then Jimmy, and five more sisters."

I added in my head and gasped, "That's nine children. Two boys."

Austin nodded. "Their father lost his job in the spring. Can you imagine trying to provide a shelter and food for nine children when you don't have a job?"

I couldn't imagine how desperate a mother and father must feel with nine children in a house. I could picture the little ones whimpering with hunger, unable to understand, and the older ones, struggling to help.

Life since the Depression started last year had had its difficult times for my family too. Papa's wrinkles had deepened as he worried how to provide for us, but God blessed us with just enough.

Austin continued. "Their father took small jobs. Their mother gardened, but it was an impossible struggle, so Jimmy was asked to move out, to find a job somewhere. The older boy, Marty, was supposed to stay and help support the family, but he couldn't stand the thought of sending his little brother alone and sneaked from the house with him. Roy came along. He's a family friend."

I frowned. "You mentioned Madison. Do you think they're heading that way?"

Austin shook his head. "Nah, I just said that to throw you off. They're not heading to Missouri either. They got no family there."

Albert leaned forward and handed his stick to Austin. "Maybe you can use this as a cane. It will help you hobble around."

"Well, thank you kindly." Austin squinted up at me. "Marty is a lot like you, Lester."

CHAPTER 13

"We were so right about Jimmy and Marty." Albert trotted beside me. "We should join the police force and help solve crimes."

I skidded to a stop. "What have we solved? We don't even know where the three boys are." I shivered again as I remembered Austin holding my hand, then comparing me to Marty. But I didn't share my fear with Albert. Instead, I crossed my arms. "We're no closer than before."

Albert backed up with his hands lifted. "I was being cheerful."

"Well, don't be." I marched toward home.

Albert shuffled along in silence, glancing sideways in my direction. I stared straight ahead.

Again Yurgi flung open the front door. "Did you find my friend, Jimmy?"

"He's not your friend," I snapped. "You never said one nice word to him." I stormed into my bedroom and slammed the door.

I needed to think without people talking to me, especially Albert and Yurgi who always had one more thing to say. I flopped onto the bed that I shared with Alya and studied the cracks in the ceiling. *Dear God, help me with this mess.* My thoughts swirled.

I grabbed my pillow and hugged it. Why would Austin stutter my boy name and then comment on my tiny hand? Did Austin think I was a girl? What did he mean when he said Marty was like me *?* If Austin thought I was a girl, he must think that Marty was too.

I bolted up. He was trying to give me more clues without telling anyone else, even Albert. If Marty was a girl and others found out, she could be in serious danger living in hobo jungles with desperate men.

I scooted off the bed. What should I do? I fluffed my hair and opened the bedroom door. The living room was empty. Soft conversation drifted from the kitchen, and I walked toward it. I couldn't tell Albert. He spoke before thinking. I couldn't tell Papa or Taty or Alya. They would worry too much. I couldn't tell Yurgi because the whole school would know on Monday. But I wished I could talk to someone.

Papa stood in the doorway with his arms crossed. "There's a little boy here who deserves an apology." Papa tipped his head toward Yurgi.

Yurgi stomped to me and glared up with big eyes. "Lis, you made me cry. I didn't feel like your little Yurgi anymore."

I scooped him up in a hug. "I'm sorry. You'll always be my little Yurgi." He squeezed me extra tight. I squeezed him tighter.

My family and Albert, plus sweet John, sat the table. He had been Johannes, a boy my age on the oxen cart as we escaped Russia. Now we called him John. He sat with his back to me.

Albert jumped up. I nodded but kept my mouth clamped shut. I could not talk to him now. He slumped back down.

John turned around. "Hello, Lis, I dropped in for a visit. Your family, well, mostly Yurgi, told me about your adventures."

Everyone around the table chuckled.

John grinned. "Albert explained about Soup Saturday and meeting Austin."

I pulled an extra chair over to the table and sat beside John, shaking my head. "The past few days have been exciting and sad. I wish we knew where the young hobos are hiding."

"Less than a year ago, I was a young hobo," John said. "Remember? You and Albert saved me from the hobo jungle. You probably saved my life. Maybe now I can help you save three more homeless boys. Let me know how I can help."

I patted John's arm. Of course. Who better than John? He had suffered much in Russia and had lived the hobo life in America. *Thank you, God, for sending John.* I would tell him my secret.

But he left with Albert before I could.

CHAPTER 14

Sunday

Every Sunday our whole family walked to church together, unless the weather was bad. Then Heinrich and Rachel gave us a ride. Even though it was mid-October, the bright sunshine warmed us as we skipped down our front steps. Alya held Taty's hand. Yurgi swung between Papa and me, jumped free, and stared down the dirt lane toward the hobo jungle. "I'm keeping watch. Every day I'll look for my new friend, Jimmy." He clapped his hand over his mouth. "I mean, he's going to be my friend, Lis. I just know it."

Papa laughed and grabbed Yurgi's hand again. "You will make a wonderful friend." Yurgi took my hand, too, and swung between us again.

I would also be keeping watch for the young hobos. I studied the riverbank as we crossed the bridge, hoping for a glimpse of them, praying we would find them.

Papa turned toward me. "You have been quiet since you and Albert returned from the hobo jungle yesterday." Papa frowned.

"Sometimes we just have to be patient and wait for God's timing. Is there more to your story than you're telling?"

Yurgi quit swinging and stared up. "Lis, you know you can tell us anything."

Papa laughed. "Or you can just tell me."

"Papa, you know if I have to tell you something, I will. For now, I have nothing to tell." I forced a grin. I did need to tell John.

Papa faced ahead, a slight frown on his face. I did the same. We walked on.

The bells of St. Peter's Lutheran Church gonged and clanged as we scrambled up the front steps and into our pews. Papa and Yurgi sat on the right side, with the men. Taty, Alya, and I went to the left. This was the old way, men on one side and women on the other. We attended the German service where we could relax with the familiar words of our first language. Ja, I knew English now, but German was still easier.

The organ blasted out the introduction for the first hymn. Alya sat between Taty and me. She nudged my leg with her knee and held the hymnal open. While my mind had drifted, she had found the first hymn, "If God Had Not Been on Our Side."

Alya pointed to the small names on the bottom of the hymn. "See? Martin Luther wrote it. We're learning about him in school. Do you think Marty's name is really Martin? Maybe he was named for Martin Luther."

I nodded, my mind again swirling. Maybe I was wrong. Maybe Marty was a boy whose name was Martin. I was so confused.

Alya tapped the hymnal and whispered, "Time to sing."

I sang, trying to focus on the words:

If God had not been on our side

And had not come to aid us,

Our foes with all their pow'r and pride

Would surely have dismayed us,

For we, his flock, would have to fear

The devil's wolves, both far and near,

Who rise in might against us.

The congregation continued singing, but I silently read the first line again. "If God had not been on our side and had not come to aid us." Ja, God was on our side, and he was helping us. I leaned back on the pew. He was helping me. As Papa said, I just had to be patient.

Alya nudged me again and tapped the last line. I jumped to join the singing, "Our helper and our strength is he who made the earth and heavens."

After church we gathered with friends on the sidewalk, absorbing the warmth of the day. I chatted with Max and Hildy until I spied John and Albert crossing the street, already walking away.

"See you tomorrow," I said to the twins and raced off. "John. Albert. Wait for me."

They swung around, shoulder to shoulder.

"Good morning, Lis," John said.

"What's up?" Albert kicked a stone. "I don't have time to chat because I have a delivery to make." He scowled and hurried away.

I called after him. "Albert, will I see you this afternoon at the prayer meeting?"

"Maybe." He waggled his head.

"What's wrong with him?"

"He'll be fine." John shrugged one shoulder. "He's still upset by how you treated him yesterday."

I hung my head. "Ja, I was confused by what was happening with the young hobos, and I treated everybody badly. Most of the time I love Albert's take-charge ways, but not all the time. I will apologize later."

Then I realized I had John all to myself. I could tell him my worries about Marty. I could share my burden with him.

As I told John my suspicions, his eyes never left my face. "I think I can help," he said.

Thank You, God, for coming to my aid. Now please give me patience to wait for You—and John.

CHAPTER 15

Monday

On Monday morning, Taty whispered in my ear. "Lisenka, dear, it's 5 a.m., time to wake up."

I rolled over and pulled the homemade quilt over my head. "It's too early. The sun isn't even up yet."

She sat on the bed and shook my shoulder. "Please get up. We don't want to wake Alya and Yurgi yet."

I sighed and slipped from under the quilt. "That's for sure," I whispered. "Especially Yurgi. I need a quiet hour to wake up myself."

Taty touched my cheek and tiptoed out.

I wriggled into my dress, tied my apron around my waist, and followed her into the kitchen. Papa was there, slicing bread for sandwiches.

"Good morning, Lis." Papa dipped a knife into the lard bucket, spread the white paste onto five thick slices of bread, sprinkled a pinch of salt on each slice, and slapped on another slice of bread. "Can you wrap them in waxed paper?"

"Sure, Papa." I cut squares of waxed paper from a big roll and wrapped up the sandwiches. "Should I get apples for each of us too?" At Papa's nod, I went down the steps, past the backdoor, and down more steps into the cellar. I held onto the damp wall until my eyes adjusted, then grabbed five apples from the bin, apples from our orchard, cradled them in my apron, and hurried back upstairs. I didn't like the dark, musty cellar.

Taty fluttered around the kitchen, measuring an extra big portion of oatmeal from a bin in the cupboard, the one beside the flour bin. She dumped the oatmeal into a kettle of hot water, already steaming on the stove. "Lisenka, can you stir the oatmeal until it boils?"

I gave Taty's waist a squeeze and stirred the oatmeal. "Thank you for helping with the morning chores. I thought I'd be on my own this morning."

"We just wanted to make sure you had a good start to your day." Papa slipped on his jacket.

"Good and early." I giggled.

Taty took off her apron and hung it on the hook by the backdoor. She grabbed her beige coat off another hook and fumbled to button it. "I don't know what's wrong with me." Her hands were trembling.

"Let me help you, Taty." I buttoned her coat and pulled her in for a hug. "Don't be nervous about your new job. You'll do great. Remember, you're an excellent seamstress."

She gave me a weak smile. "Are you sure you'll be fine with getting the three of you to school?"

"I'm sure."

After they went out the front door, I stirred the oatmeal again, scooted the kettle off the hot stove to let the oatmeal soften, and sank down at the kitchen table, breathing in a short-lived moment of quiet. It was interrupted by a soft tapping on the backdoor. My heart leaped in my chest and pounded as I crept down the steps and pulled aside the curtain on the window to peek out.

"John!" I flung open the door.

"Shhh!" He put his finger to his lips. "I saw your parents leave. Are the little ones still asleep?"

I nodded.

He turned and motioned into the darkness. I strained to see where he gazed. Three shadows crept from behind the chicken coop. As they moved into the circle of light from our door, I slapped my hands to my chest.

"John, where did you find them?"

"Shh!" John said again. "I wore my raggedy clothes, smeared dirt on my face, and spent the night at the hobo jungle near Five Corners. After dark, I saw them creep into camp and huddle near the fire. I waited until everyone drifted off to bedrolls, blankets, or cardboard boxes. Then I talked to them, telling them about you, Albert, and your family."

As the three hesitated a few feet from the door, I forced a smile. "Hello Marty, Jimmy, and Roy."

Their strained faces relaxed. I was happy to see them, but I didn't move.

"Lisenka." John slapped his arms. "Are you going to invite us in? We're freezing out here. And we don't want the neighbors to see us."

"Ja, yes, sorry." I stepped back. John held the door open while the young hobos followed me up the steps and into our kitchen. They headed for the warmth of our wood-burning stove, rubbing hands together.

John tugged me aside. "Marty is still a mystery. He never wavered in his disguise, if it is one." he whispered. "For now, they need our help. Do you think they could stay here today?"

"Today? I have to go to school. I can't skip school. Eddy will be angry if I waste his money and skip out."

"What if I stay here with them, take a sick day from work. These poor people need to warm up, eat up, and clean up."

I chewed on my bottom lip, considering. But I couldn't consider anything long because I had to get the little ones and me ready for school.

CHAPTER 16

As usual, Yurgi stood watch in the front room. "Max and Hildy are here," he called.

I stacked the last clean bowl on the shelf, grabbed our lunch pails, and glanced around the kitchen. Everything looked normal, except for a second kettle of oatmeal simmering on the stove, except for John peeking from the cellar steps.

"Taty and Papa will be home after 1 p.m.," I whispered. "Be sure to clean up and be gone by then."

John gave a nod as I hurried from the kitchen.

"Alya, are you ready?" I stopped at our room.

She was struggling to tie her hair ribbon. "I can't get it."

"I can." And I did. "Here's your lunch pail. Yurgi, here's your lunch too."

"Good morning, Lis," Max gave me a dignified nod as Yurgi and Alya skipped ahead of me down the steps. "I trust you had a nice weekend. I wrote my entire research paper."

"Really, Max?" Hildy elbowed ahead and pulled me along. She called over her shoulder. "Do you have to brag so early in the morning?"

"That wasn't bragging." Max hurried to catch up. "I was trying to inspire Lis to keep up with her studies."

"You are impossible."

"I am not."

I shoved my hands in my jacket pockets and kept walking. When we turned the corner onto Main Street, Officer Kowalaski strolled toward us. "Good morning, children. Is everything fine today?"

"Good morning, officer," Yurgi yelled. "Let me know if you need any help solving crimes."

Officer Kowalski touched his hat and continued on his beat.

I shook my head. How could it be a normal Monday morning for everyone except me? I had three young hobos hiding in our basement. And a full school day to worry what we were going to do with them.

+ + + + +

As the five of us walked home from school, John joined us. "I have to talk to you, Lisenka." He refused to use the American name I wanted, especially when there was trouble.

"You are just the person I wanted to see, Johannes." I used his German name too.

"I know." He grimaced.

Max stepped between us. "First it's Albert. Now it's John. Why do you want to see him when you're with me?"

Poor Max. I patted his arm. "John and I are working on a project together. Do you mind if we drop back a little so we can talk?"

Max exhaled and rubbed his jaw. "Well, fine then. Come along, children." He hurried the little ones ahead, acting like the teacher he hoped to be. Hildy shrugged and sprinted to join them.

"Did you find a shelter for Marty, Jimmy, and Roy?"

John grabbed my arm. "They are still in your cellar."

"What? You were supposed to feed them, wash them up, and move them."

"I know. I did feed them and heat a kettle of water for them to wash their hands and faces. After we all cleaned up the kitchen, we sat around the table. Their sad eyes stared at the ceiling, at the floor, anywhere but at me. Finally, I glanced from one to the other and asked, 'How can I help you?'

"Marty answered, 'Roy and I don't need help, but we're worried about Jimmy. He's gotten skinnier, and he's starting to cough. We're afraid to ask for help. If the authorities discover that we're homeless and have a ten-year-old child with us, Jimmy will be taken away to live in an orphanage.' Marty shuddered. 'I hear they're horrible.'"

"So that's why they're hiding," As Marty's words sank into my head, I stared at a falling leaf. When it floated onto the sidewalk, I asked, "Where are Taty and Papa?"

"They're home, suspecting nothing, I hope. Before 1 p.m., I gathered some quilts from your closet and settled Marty, Roy, and Jimmy in the back corner of your cellar, behind the potato bins. Lucky for me, I glanced out the window and saw your parents walk up the sidewalk. They were earlier than I expected, but I was ready. When they opened the front door, I slipped out and locked the backdoor."

"Whew." I blew out a big breath. "Well, at least we know our young hobos are safe, but what a mess we have here. I don't know what to do."

CHAPTER 17

W e walked on in silence. A block ahead, Yurgi and Alya waved goodbye to Max and Hildy and skipped into our house. Max turned back and gave me a little wave and a big idea.

I swung John around to face me. "Max and Hildy's grandma, Frau Brunhild, gave me a home when we first moved to Fond du Lac. Heinrich and Rachel took in Taty and the little ones. Somebody else housed Papa."

John's eyes brightened. "And Albert's family took me. I'm still there, paying room and board now."

He tapped his jaw. "My job at Sadoff Iron Works is going well. Maybe I could get an apartment and take care of all three."

I arched my eyebrows. "Now you're sounding like Albert, solving all the world's problems by yourself. John, that is very kind, but we can't wait. We need a solution now. What if we find one or two different families to take them in?"

"Good idea. Our friends might help."

"Let's start with Papa and Taty."

"Papa! Taty!" I yelled as we slammed through the front door. "We need to talk." But when we stepped through the living room, all thoughts of helping the young hobos flew from my head. Someone was crying. I hurried to the kitchen doorway and froze there, lifting one hand to stop John behind me.

Taty sat on a chair, her head in her arms on the table. Deep sobs shook her body. Papa knelt beside her with his arm around her back. Yurgi patted her shoulder. Alya stood still, wringing her hands, tears streaming down her cheeks.

"What's wrong?" I gasped.

Papa glanced up. His eyes were red with sadness. "Taty cut her thumb at work today. Her supervisor, Mr. Luczak, yelled at her for her clumsiness and said not to come back until it is healed."

Taty sat up and showed us her thumb. It was wrapped in a big white bandage. "I was proud to take my seat with the rest of the cutters this morning." Taty hiccupped. "We all sit at a long table. A roll of sock tops was brought to each of us from the ribbing department. We were to cut each sock top apart from our roll, using two little blades."

Papa stood up and crossed his arms. "But the supervisors are more interested in fast work than in properly training the new workers."

Taty stretched her shoulders. "A sweet lady who sat next to me helped. I was doing fine, cutting and trimming. She also showed me how to put two tops together and roll them inside out, then drop them into a basket at my feet. As soon as we had reached our quota, twenty-four in the basket, we raised our hand for a runner to pick them up."

Papa smiled at Taty. "Occasionally, I glanced in to check on her. Such an intent little lady she was, trying hard to do a good job."

Taty flashed Papa a grateful smile. "But that supervisor paced back and forth behind my chair, saying, 'Pick up your pace, lady. You'll never reach your quota for the day.' Do you remember, Lisenka, how nervous I was before the day began? His yelling just made me shake more."

Taty sighed. "Near the end of my shift, my back was stiff from sitting so long, and my eyes were bleary from squinting at the tiny threads. Just for a moment, I glanced away from my work. I don't know what happened. When I looked back, blood was dripping on the sock in my hand. I had sliced my thumb on the sharp cutter." Taty shuddered with another sob.

"The supervisor charged over, yelling that I would have to pay for the ruined sock. Of course I would pay for what I ruined. I used my handkerchief to wipe up the blood on my table and then tied it around my thumb." Taty rubbed her hand over her pale face.

Papa took over her story. "Not only is Taty embarrassed that she didn't finish her first day of work, but she is worried Infant Socks might give her position to someone else."

"I know I can do the work." Taty held up her thumb. "Hopefully, my job will still be there next week when this silly bandage comes off."

Papa studied John and me, standing in the doorway, our feet stuck to the floor. "Lis and John, why don't you come in and sit down?"

We slid into chairs across the table. "Taty, you had a terrible first day."

"Ja, it was terrible, but I liked learning new skills and chatting a bit with other ladies nearby. I can't be fired."

I focused on a crack in the ceiling, wondering how I could help Taty, then I bolted up. "I have sewing skills. What if I fill in for you for a few days?"

CHAPTER 18

John was the first to react to my kind but stupid idea. He grabbed my arm. "Lisenka, don't you have enough to do already?" He glared at me and squeezed my arm. His frowning face loomed closer, reminding me we had other problems, and they were hiding in our cellar.

Taty patted my hand. "Lisenka, I can't let you give up school for a week. What will Eddy say?"

John nodded at Taty. "That's right." He squeezed my arm tighter. "Your job is going to school. Eddy will not be happy if you skip out."

I settled back in my chair, sorry I had blurted out my idea, sorry I had forgotten about the people in our cellar, sorry I always rushed ahead without thinking.

But I didn't know how to take back my words, and so I bumbled on. "Maybe Eddy will understand if I promise to go to school every afternoon after one o'clock and keep up with all my studies. Max will help me with that."

Out of the corner of my eye, I glimpsed John's slight shake of his head.

Taty glanced from John to me. "John's right. I can't let you give up your life to fix my mistakes."

Papa stood and paced back and forth. "Let's think about this a little." As he paced more, a train rumbled past across the street. "Lis might be on the right track."

I raised one eyebrow. "A word joke now, Papa?"

He winked at me. I could count on Papa to make me smile, but he turned serious again. "Here's an idea. What if I take Lis along to Infant Socks in the morning and introduce her to Mr. Luczak? We can at least see what he says. If he says no, she heads to school. If he says yes, Lis will begin work. Maybe if he sees us trying to take care of Taty's job, he might be more likely to welcome her back."

Taty's tight face relaxed. "Maybe we could give it a try. Lisenka, thank you for your kind offer. You are a blessing to me."

Under the table, John bumped his knee into mine. I cleared my throat and scooted my chair back. "Well, then, it's settled. I'll work for Taty tomorrow. Now would you all excuse John and me? We have to talk about a little project."

Yurgi jumped up and grabbed my hand. "May I help with your project, Lis?"

I peeled off his little hand. "Not yet. But I'm pretty sure you'll be helping soon."

He lifted his chin. "Just let me know what I have to do."

I pressed my hand against John's back and pushed him toward the front door. As it slammed behind us, I whispered, "Now what?"

John's eyes grew big. "You're asking me that after you complicate our lives with working at Infant Socks?"

I sank onto the front step, resting my head on my knees. "I had to help Taty. You saw how miserable she was. How does working at Infant Socks change anything?"

John settled down beside me. "Well, actually it complicates your life, not mine. The household drama over Infant Socks has settled down. Now we have to do something about Marty, Jimmy, and Roy. We can't keep them hidden in your cellar all night until we work out a plan. Besides, Taty will be home alone tomorrow. We don't know them well enough to trust them in the house with just Taty."

"I don't want them to spend the night in the dark, damp cellar either." I slapped my knees and stood up. "Let's return to our first plan. We need ask for help with this project. Won't Yurgi be thrilled?"

+ + + + +

I stood by the stove while John scooted past and down the cellar steps. Yurgi ran around the table and hugged me. "Are you ready for my help with your project, Lis?"

I hugged him back and took a deep breath. "Ja, we're ready for all of you to help. Papa and Taty, you say we can tell you anything. Well, we have something to talk about."

John led the three hobos into the kitchen, then stepped aside, standing between them and the backdoor. Marty, Jimmy, and Roy squinted in the bright light and cowered together in a clump. Their faces and hands glowed from John's wash-up duty this morning. They were wrapped in familiar quilts from my closet, but their dirty clothes hung from their skinny bodies. Marty crossed his arms. The other two hung their heads.

Taty gasped and covered her mouth with her hands. "Were they in our cellar all afternoon?"

Papa jumped up, sending his chair clattering backwards. "Lis and John, you have some explaining to do."

Alya screamed and wrapped her arms around Taty's neck, but Yurgi clapped his hands. He wiggled from my hug and ran to the little boy. "Jimmy, I'm happy to see you again. If you promise to not steal Rosie, we can be friends."

CHAPTER 19

Papa crossed his arms and tapped his foot. I turned away and grabbed the kettle, pumped water into it, and slid it onto the stovetop. "I'll make tea for our meeting."

Papa stepped closer. "Meeting? Who called a meeting?"

While I squirmed to answer, Yurgi stared up at Papa. "It's a prayer meeting, Papa. God calls us to prayer meetings every Sunday afternoon. Can't we have one on Monday evening too?"

Papa rubbed his hands together. "A prayer meeting? Well, ja, I suppose we should have a prayer meeting." He scratched his head. "This situation does indeed need prayer, but how should we start?"

Alya unwound her arms from Taty's neck and studied the little-boy hobo. He gave Alya a wobbly grin, and she grinned back. Then she turned to Papa. "May we talk about God's Golden Rule, the one in Matthew 7:12? You mentioned it last week. Remember? I memorized it in school today."

I glanced from Yurgi to Papa to Alya. How was it that this meeting was happening without me? "What is that rule?"

Alya took a deep breath. "Do for others whatever you want people to do for you."

"Thank you, Alya." Papa patted her head. "Having hobos hiding in my cellar was such a shock I forgot about that Bible passage for a moment." He glanced at me. I bent over the kettle, my eyes on the water, as I sprinkled tea leaves into it.

Papa walked up to me and turned me to face him. "Lis, thanks for thinking of others. Please pull up more chairs for our guests and have a seat. Alya can finish making the tea."

Papa glanced at John. "Thank you, too, young man. Please close the backdoor and escort our guests to the table."

With tenderness, John nudged Marty, Jimmy, and Roy to the chairs I'd pulled up. Then he sat down and patted the chair next to him. I sank into it. Yurgi climbed onto my lap.

"Let's begin with a prayer," Papa said. I folded my hands over Yurgi's. Our guests folded theirs too. "Lord, thank You for bringing these poor young people into our kitchen. Please guide us as we discuss how we can help them. We know You love them and have a plan for them. Show us what to do. We pray for healing for their bodies and their souls. Amen."

Our amens echoed around the table.

Taty studied her skinny guests. "First, we eat. Pavel, please get the ham platter from the icebox. Thanks for slicing it off the bone while I sat here crying this afternoon. Lisenka, get a loaf of bread, the crock of butter, and a jar of strawberry jam."

While I sliced the bread, Alya set down plates and table knives and passed out the thick slices of bread. We helped ourselves to the rest.

As soon as everyone was served and the tea was steeping, Papa turned to John and me. "You both have a story to tell."

We told our story while our young hobos devoured most of the food. As we described the past few days, they leaned back. When I mentioned Yurgi's make-believe friendship with Jimmy, Marty glanced at Roy and chuckled.

Papa stood again. "Thank you, Lis and John, for not giving up on Marty, Jimmy, and Roy, and for bringing them here for help." Papa raised one eyebrow. "Even though it would have been nice to know earlier that people were hiding in our cellar."

John and I grinned at each other.

Papa studied Marty, Jimmy, and Roy. Marty's eyes darted back and forth like a cornered rabbit. He tugged his stocking hat lower.

Papa paced behind his chair. "Martin, you seem to be in charge of the group. We'd like to hear your story."

Jimmy jumped up and slapped the table. "Her name ain't Martin. It's Martha."

Marty gasped and yanked Jimmy back down. But it was too late. Her secret was out. She peeled off her tattered, gray stocking hat. Stringy blonde hair fell to her shoulders, a stark contrast to her dark eyes.

"Martha?" I also jumped up. "I knew it. Austin knew you were a girl too."

Roy turned to Marty. A frown puckered her forehead, and she shrugged one shoulder. Roy asked, "Who's Austin? We don't know anyone named Austin."

CHAPTER 20

Albert yelled from the front door. "Hello?"

"Come in!" Yurgi ran to meet him in the living room and pulled him toward the kitchen. "You won't believe who is here again." Yurgi stood in the doorway and flung his arm toward the kitchen.

Albert lowered Yurgi's hand so he could pass through but skidded to a stop when he spied our guests. "Where did you find them? I thought they were long gone."

John shrugged. "I guess it takes a hobo to find a hobo."

Albert glanced from one hobo to the next. Then his head snapped back to stare at Marty. "Wait a minute. Is he a she?"

John stood and pushed his chair toward Albert. "Sure is. Her name is Martha. You better take a seat."

After Albert sank into his chair, I leaned toward him. "I'm sorry I was rude on Saturday. Austin worried me, especially when he commented on my small hand and then said I was like Marty. I was afraid of what he meant."

"Oh, you already suspected that Marty was a girl?"

I nodded. "I didn't want to tell you or anyone until I was sure. But my head was pounding, trying to keep the secret. If Marty was a girl and if Austin knew it, other hobos might know too. I worried men might try to hurt her. On Sunday, I asked John to try to find them. Last night, he did."

Albert rubbed his jaw. He was, for once, speechless.

Yurgi pranced up to Albert. "They were hiding in our cellar all day, even when we were here and Mama was crying."

"Why was Taty crying?" Albert glanced at Taty, worry filling his face.

"We're past that worry," Papa said. "Now let's move to the next one. How can we find homes for Marty, Jimmy, and Roy?"

Albert straightened his shoulders. "Maybe I can help with that. I make it my business to know everyone's business." He gave me a sideways glance. "Some people call it being nosy."

I squeezed my eyes shut. "Albert, are you trying to take over again?"

"It's in my nature, Lis, to react fast. I'm trying to relax." His speech slowed to a turtle pace. "Are we looking for three homes for three people?"

"That might be the easiest," Papa said. "Our friends will be more likely to take in one person rather than two or three."

Marty tapped the table. "You didn't let us tell our story. Jimmy is my little brother. When he was kicked out of our house, I went with him. I'm not deserting him now. Where he goes, I go. If that's impossible, we're moving on."

"Thanks, Marty." Jimmy leaned against her.

I studied the three young hobos. "This is so confusing. Austin said Jimmy was your little brother. How would he know that?"

"Look, Lis or Lisenka or whoever you are. Quit making up stories. We do not know Austin," Marty said.

Albert glared at Marty. "Watch how you talk to my friend. She's not making up a story. We both met Austin. He's real, and he knows about you."

Marty nibbled on a fingernail and whispered, "How could this man know about us unless he's been spying on us, listening to our private conversations? I'm scared."

"He seemed friendly, but who knows?" Albert said. "For now, it's really important that we find safe places for you to stay."

Papa leaned forward. "Safe is right. Let's talk this through." He turned to Marty. "So you two need to stay together in whatever home we find, right?"

She nodded. Tears filled her eyes. "It would sure be nice if Roy could stay with us too. He's been there for us every day since we left home. We couldn't have survived without him."

"Is he a cousin? A family friend?" I asked.

"My fiancée."

CHAPTER 21

Papa blew out a breath and studied Roy. "How old are you, young man?"

"I'm nineteen, sir."

"Do you think it's proper for you to be traveling with your fiancée without a chaperone?"

Roy stared into Papa's eyes. "We didn't have a choice, but don't worry. I respect Marty too much to take advantage of her."

Papa continued to stare at Roy.

Roy met his stare. "This is not the life I planned for us." Roy blinked several times. "How could I let Marty and Jimmy run away and not come along to protect them? I work in home construction and thought I'd find a job as we traveled, find a justice of the peace to marry us, and settle down with Marty and Jimmy."

Marty reached for Roy's hand. "We want to get married, but our lives have gone from bad to desperate. We need jobs. We need food. Now that it's getting cold, we need a place to live. Jimmy needs to get strong again and go back to school. We need so much, but we're stuck in homelessness. Life is a dead end for us." A sob caught in her throat. She covered her eyes with one hand.

"Why would God give us this life?" Roy asked. "What kind of loving God would put us in this hopeless situation?"

The mantle clock ticked. Nobody spoke for a minute.

Then Papa's soft words broke the silence. "Our loving God brought you to us. Now how can we help you?"

We all talked at once.

"Heinrich and Rachel might help."

"Frau Brunhild has extra rooms and might take two."

"We could ask the pastor if he knows of a room for Roy."

"Can you think of anybody who could take three?"

We all had questions, but nobody had an answer except Yurgi. He was loudest. "Jimmy can stay with me. There's room in my bed for him to sleep." He glanced at Marty. "But she won't fit in Lis and Alya's bed. It's already crowded."

Papa shushed Yurgi. "We don't have room here. Marty and Jimmy should stay together, but the question is where?"

"I agree with Yurgi." Taty pushed a dirty plate aside. "They could stay with us for tonight at least, until we find something permanent for them."

Yurgi flashed Taty a knowing grin but studied Jimmy. "He can't sleep in my bed with those dirty clothes, can he?"

Jimmy brushed his mud-streaked sleeve. None of the dirt budged. His bottom lip quivered. "Don't reckon I can do anything about my clothes. This is all I got."

Roy hung his head. "Jimmy is right. We have no other clothes and no way of buying any."

I slid my chair back. "I know where to go to solve the clothes problem. Come on, Albert and John. Let's visit Eddy Monroe."

CHAPTER 22

"Wouldn't it be nice to own an automobile?" Albert asked on our twenty-minute walk to Eddy's house on Division Street. "I've already pushed my delivery cart all over town today. I'm tired."

"I'm definitely tired of walking everywhere I want to go." John limped, trying to keep up. My thoughts drifted to our escape from Russia three years ago, when the oxen cart wheel rolled over John's foot and smashed it. His limp got worse when he was tired.

"Maybe we can buy an old automobile together," Albert said.

"That's a great idea." John spun to a stop. "Split costs and share rides."

I ran ahead to face them. "Maybe I could pay you to give me rides, too, or better yet, you could give me rides for free. Maybe after you learn to drive, you can teach me."

"You?" Both boys gaped at me.

"Girls don't drive." Albert shook his finger. "It's just too dangerous."

I lifted my head. Bossy Albert was at it again.

Our banter had carried us all the way to Eddy's big house. We circled to the backdoor, the entrance I always used when I worked for his mother, and we pounded with the brass knocker.

When I heard footsteps approaching, my heart raced. I was nervous because besides begging for hand-me-down clothes, I also had to explain my adjusted school schedule to Eddy. He was not an easy person to convince of anything.

"Well, hello, Lis, Albert, and John." Eddy's face filled with a friendly grin. "Would you like to come in?"

We were all speechless. This was not the down-to-business, never-smile Eddy that we knew.

I recovered my voice first. "Thank you, Eddy. We would."

Eddy led us into the kitchen. "Please have a seat." He motioned to the fancy chairs around the shiny oak table. "I was just making a pot of tea to go with the cookies Frau Brunhild dropped off. I pay her for a dozen cookies per week. She gets a little extra money, and I get her delicious cookies."

When we were all seated and Eddy had served us cookies and tea, I inhaled deeply. Almost without taking a second breath, I explained everything.

Eddy shook his head. "Poor Taty to have such a bad first day. Of course, you may work out the best schedule you can with Infant Socks and WLA. I trust that you will try your hardest to do well in both positions."

I glanced at Albert and John. Their eyes darted back and forth. Nothing about this was normal. I chewed my last bite of cookie and gulped down my tea.

Eddy tipped back on his chair. "And about those clothes, Lis, why don't you and your friends run upstairs and find the clothes you need? The little boy clothes are still in the baby's room, as Mother called it." He paused and grinned at me. I grinned back, remembering sweet Mrs. Monroe.

Eddy patted my hand. "We still miss her, don't we, but she'd want to share with the teenage girl. Why don't you look in Mother's closet for something for Martha."

"This is very generous of you, Eddy." I stood to go upstairs.

Eddy raised his hand. "Now what can we do for Roy? Do you think my clothes will fit him? Go ahead and check out my closet. I have too many clothes and wanted to give some away anyway."

The three of us tripped over each other in our rush up the steps. "I can't believe how sweet Eddy is," I whispered.

"Me either," John said.

"I'm going to have to find out what's going on," Albert added.

We were in the baby's room, digging through boxes, when Eddy called up the stairs. "If you hurry, I'll give you a ride home. Your house, Lis, is on my way to Abigail Meuschlin's apartment. I'm picking her up for dinner."

I dropped the shirt I'd been holding up.

An entire box of clothes slipped from Albert's hand. "So that's what's going on. My natural curiosity can relax. Could this be a romance in the making?"

CHAPTER 23

———◆━◆━◆━◆━———

Yurgi was peering out the window when we drove up. By the time we struggled up the front steps with our arms full of clothes, he was holding the door open. His body blocked most of the doorway as he stared down the street. "Was that Eddy?"

"That was the new Eddy." I squeezed between Yurgi and the open door. Albert and John pushed through too. Yurgi continued to watch Eddy's car.

"You're teasing, Lis. That was the old Eddy and his car. I wonder where he's going." Yurgi wrinkled his forehead. "Shouldn't he be at home? It's almost suppertime."

Albert, John, and I dropped our piles of clothing on the bed-couch in the living room. Albert sank onto it beside the piles of clothing and tugged Yurgi down beside him. I liked that Albert gave Yurgi extra attention. "Do you want to know where the new Eddy was going?"

Yurgi's head bobbed up and down.

"He's taking Miss Meuschlin out to eat."

Yurgi's mouth dropped open. "Are they in love?"

I straightened my back and brushed my hands together. "No, Yurgi. They are just friends. Your classmates at school don't need to know. Understand?"

Yurgi took a few seconds until he nodded.

"Well done, gentlemen." I said to Albert and John and turned toward the kitchen. "Let's see how our guests are doing."

Yurgi charged in front of me and flung his arms wide. "Stop! You can't go in there now. It's bath time."

"For all of them?" Albert gasped.

Alya stepped from our room. "No, silly. Marty's bath is done. She's in our room, wrapped in quilts. Taty is brushing her hair."

Yurgi lowered his arms, relaxing his guard duty. "The door to the kitchen is closed because now Jimmy and Roy are taking turns in the tub. Papa filled it full of hot water, just like for us on Saturday night." Yurgi scuffed his foot on the wooden floor. "And just like for us, the girls get to have a bath first."

"So Marty's ready for her clothes? Wonderful." I grabbed Mrs. Monroe's old clothes—Marty's new clothes—and knocked on our bedroom door.

"Come in," Taty called.

I dropped the pile onto Yurgi's bed and turned around. Marty and Taty perched on the edge of our bed. I gasped in surprise. "Marty, you're so pretty. How did you ever fool anyone into believing you were a young man?"

Marty blushed. "I'd do anything for Jimmy, even dress in rags."

"Well, you'll be dressed in rags no more." I held up a gold wool church dress in one hand, trimmed with lace around the neckline and wrists, and a cream-colored shawl in the other. "What do you think? We tried to pick clothes from an old woman's wardrobe that a young woman might like."

"They're beautiful."

"Church clothes are the prettiest, but we also have a blue plaid housedress, a beige sweater, two aprons, warm stockings, a flannel nightgown, long underwear, a winter coat, and flat shoes." I held up each as I spoke. Marty crossed her hands over her chest while tears streaked down her cheeks. "I can't believe these are for me."

Tears filled my eyes too. "All these clothes are yours."

"We'll give you privacy while you dress." Taty rose from the bed, put her arms around Alya and me, and nudged us from the room.

The kitchen door was open now, but shouting was coming through it. John yelled, "Hurry up, Albert. He must be heading to the hobo jungle. You're faster! You can catch him."

When the three of us rushed into the kitchen, we found only Papa, Roy, and Yurgi standing around the empty tub.

"Where's Jimmy?" I dashed into the kitchen.

"I think he's gone." Roy bit his lip. "I came out of the bedroom just now."

Papa shook his head. "He was clean and dressed in new clothes, sitting at the kitchen table. Roy was putting on his clothes in our bedroom, so I opened the kitchen door for Yurgi, invited him in to chat. Then I lugged the tub out to dump the water behind the chicken coop."

Yurgi's eyes brimmed with tears. "It's my fault. I came to talk to my new friend. Jimmy argued that he wasn't my friend. I said he was. Then he screamed in my face. 'Nobody wants me. Why should you want to be my friend?' And he ran out the back door."

Yurgi threw himself on a chair, sobbing.

Papa shook his head. "Albert and John tore out after him. Jimmy can't be that far away. I'm sure they'll find him."

Marty stood in the doorway in her blue plaid house dress. Her face blanched white. "If Jimmy doesn't want to be found, nobody will find him. We grew up roaming the woods of West Virginia. He knows how to hunt and hide. Especially hide."

CHAPTER 24

Roy reached out his hand to Marty. She ran into his arms, crying. He hugged her, swaying back and forth, until her tears stopped.

When she turned around to face the rest of us, she said, "I'm really sorry. You've shown us kindness, and we've repaid you with lies and anger."

Marty sighed. "Jimmy has a bad temper. He picked fights with us kids and sassed Ma and Pa, too, especially when they asked him to help around the house. Maybe Pa expected more of Jimmy since he was the only boy, but they often had angry words. One day, Pa screamed at him to get out. Jimmy grabbed his jacket and bolted out the door. As the door slammed behind him, he shouted, 'I ain't never coming back. I hate you all.'"

Marty sank into a chair and squeezed her eyes shut. "We knew he meant it. His stupid pride wouldn't let him back down, but when I saw Ma collapse to the floor and Pa stand there with his big hands hanging limp, I needed to try."

Roy continued the story. "Of course, Marty found Jimmy. She knew his tricks, but when he refused to go home, she brought him to my house. We decided to run away together and start a wonderful new life."

Roy sat in the chair beside Marty and patted her back. "That hasn't worked out so well for us."

Albert rushed through the backdoor. "Did Jimmy come back?" He jogged up the steps to the kitchen.

We shook our heads.

John stepped into the doorway. "How can one little boy disappear that fast? We searched the hobo jungle and checked the riverbanks. Nothing."

"But it's dark out now, almost impossible to see into every nook and shadow." Albert sighed.

"Poof." Yurgi swung his hands up. "He's gone."

"No, he's not. He's not running far. When you run, you get caught. I know he's hiding. I must go after him now." Marty rubbed her hands down her new dress. "But I can't go in these clothes. Where are my hobo clothes? I need them back."

Papa peeked into the wood-burning stove. "Well, that's not going to happen. I burned those old rags. They're nothing but a pile of ashes now."

Marty's shoulders slumped. "Oh no, I have to follow Jimmy soon, or I'll lose his trail. What can I wear?"

I tapped my cheek for a second. "Come with me, Marty. I have just what you need."

Shortly, Marty walked back into the kitchen dressed in my hobo clothes, a slight grin on her face. "I remember seeing a hobo who looked like this serving soup at the hobo jungle a couple days ago."

"You were there?" I gasped.

"Yep, but we didn't trust you enough to come out of our hiding place."

I glanced at Albert. He shrugged. "My Saturday soup plan almost worked."

Roy headed toward the door. "Let's go."

"Maybe I should go alone." Marty gazed at his worried face. "Jimmy might run away from you."

"You're not going alone." Roy tugged her toward the door. "We've been our own little family for two months already. I'm not leaving you now."

As the backdoor slammed behind them, I yelled, "Are you coming back?"

Nobody answered.

"We can't just sit here, waiting," Papa said. "Taty, you and Alya stay here in case Jimmy comes back. Lis and John, you search the streets north of here. Albert, head east on Johnson Street and circle back on Division. I'll look to the south and west."

"Papa, you're forgetting me." Yurgi pulled on Papa's sleeve.

Papa swept him up and twirled around. "I will never forget you, son. Even if I get upset with you, please remember I will always love you."

Yurgi patted Papa's whiskers. "I will always love you too. But how can I help?"

I tugged Yurgi from Papa's arms. "Yurgi, would you like to help John and me?"

CHAPTER 25

We trudged north on Brooke Street, calling for Jimmy, peering between houses, peeking under bushes. Nothing. Just then, Eddy's automobile eased to a stop beside us. He opened his window. "Hey, kids, what are you doing walking out here after dark?"

I dashed to Eddy's automobile. "We're searching for Jimmy. He ran away." I tried to control a sob. "He was clean and dressed in your cute ten-year-old clothes. Something snapped in his head when Yurgi tried to be his friend, and he bolted out the door."

"We're all looking for him on the blocks around Brooke Street, but he could be anywhere, hiding in the shadows," John said. "We could walk right past him and not even know it."

Eddy nodded. "Yes, it could be pointless walking the streets. He'll be watching for you and duck into a bush or behind a house. Why don't you jump in the back seat, and we'll cruise around a bit. He won't be expecting you to be in an automobile."

As Eddy slowly drove up and down the streets, John, Yurgi, and I strained to see into every shadow.

"What's that? Something moved over there." I pointed to the right by a bush. Eddy screeched to a stop. We all squinted in that direction. A dog was digging in an empty yard.

"A dog!" Yurgi jumped up and opened the window. "Hey, dog! You want to be my dog?"

"It's probably a runaway." Eddy shifted into gear and let the automobile roll along.

"Shouldn't we take that poor dog home?" Yurgi peeked out the back window.

Eddy turned and grinned at me in the back seat. "That's an idea. You seem to be good at taking in strays."

I glared at Eddy and gently turned Yurgi around. "He has a home already, right there." I glanced back as the dog spun around, put his nose to the ground, and ran behind the house.

After a few more minutes, Eddy turned the car toward home. "We've been searching for a half hour. Arndt Street is pretty far for Jimmy to run. I don't think we'll find him if he doesn't want to be found."

I sank back on the seat. "It's dark and cold, cold enough to snow tonight. What was Jimmy thinking to run away from our warm house?"

"He wasn't thinking, Lis." John put his hand over mine, resting on the padded seat.

Eddy glanced back at us. "He's an angry young boy, running away from more than you and your family. Sometimes I felt that way as a young boy, trying to please my dad. Don't worry. He's smart and has enough spunk to survive."

We pulled in front of our house as Heinrich and Rachel parked their automobile across the street. Papa crawled out.

"I see you found a helper too. Thanks, Eddy," Papa said as we slid from Eddy's automobile. "Did you find anything?"

"Nothing, Papa."

"Unless you want to add a stray dog to your family." Eddy winked.

"Could we have the dog, Papa, please?" Yurgi jumped up and down, tugging on Papa's coat.

"We can't afford to feed a dog." Papa glared at Eddy, then ducked down to peek into Heinrich's automobile. "We appreciate your help, Heinrich and Rachel."

"That's what friends are for," Heinrich said. "Rachel and I drive around every night looking for friends who need a ride."

Rachel gave Heinrich a playful slap on his arm. "People never know when you're joking or serious, Heinrich. What am I going to do with you?"

Heinrich chuckled and squeezed her hand. Rachel's dimples deepened as she turned to Papa. "We're grateful we saw you as we were driving home from Frau Brunhild's house. We're sorry we didn't find the runaway boy. If I were his mama, I'd be very worried."

Papa nodded. "Why don't you folks come in for a cup of hot tea?" He turned back to Eddy. "Please join us, Eddy. Maybe all of us can talk our way through whatever's going on."

As our expanding search crew climbed the front steps and crowded into the living room, Taty and Alya dashed in from the kitchen, hopeful smiles on their faces. "Did you find Jimmy?"

"No." I closed the door.

Taty walked closer. "Did you see Roy and Marty?"

"No." Papa headed toward the kitchen.

A soft knock sounded. Albert swung the door open, shaking his head. "I found nothing but this stray dog." He pointed out the door to a gold-colored, long-haired mutt. "When I walked up, she was sitting there, staring at the door, and didn't budge as I passed by her."

We crowded around the open door.

"That's the same dog," I gasped. "She must have followed Eddy's automobile home."

The dog sat on the sidewalk, staring up at us. Her big brown eyes blinked once. Yurgi squeezed past us. "I love her!" He dashed down the steps.

"Stop, Yurgi." I grabbed for his jacket but missed. "She could bite you."

Yurgi didn't stop. He didn't even hesitate, just threw his arms around the dog and grinned up at us. "I'm naming her Goldy."

"Her name is not Goldy." I took one step down and pointed to the dog. "She probably already has a name and belongs to the people who live in that house on Arndt Street."

"No, Papa, no." Tears filled Yurgi's eyes. "Can't we keep Goldy?"

CHAPTER 26

I held my breath, waiting for Papa's answer. Instead, he turned to Eddy. "Can you remember where that house is? We need to return Goldy—I mean, this dog—right now."

Eddy glanced from the dog to Yurgi. "I do remember the house. There was a vacant lot beside it with overgrown bushes and weeds. I have a soft rope in the trunk. Let's tie that around Goldy's neck so she can't run away."

While Eddy got the rope, we encircled Yurgi and Goldy. Papa knelt down beside Yurgi. "She really is a beautiful dog." He petted her soft fur. "I think she's a golden retriever."

Yurgi sniffed and rubbed his eyes. "She's my friend."

When Eddy returned with the rope, he glanced at Yurgi's flushed face. "Why don't we go see if anyone knows Goldy. You can hold onto her in the backseat for me."

Yurgi leaped up and gently led the dog toward Eddy's automobile. "Come on, girl. We're going to take a little ride, but don't worry. I know you're mine."

Eddy and Yurgi were gone quite a while. Heinrich and Rachel had said their good-byes. Albert and John left to scan the hobo jungle again, and the rest of us were seated around the kitchen table, sipping lukewarm tea.

Taty stared at Papa. "Don't you think they've been gone too long?"

Papa grinned. "You know Eddy. He will be thorough in his search."

Just then, Yurgi burst through the backdoor, firmly holding Goldy's rope. He skidded to a stop below the steps and folded his hands against his chest. "Please! Please! Papa and Mama, may I keep her? Nobody on Arndt Street knows her."

Eddy scooted in behind Yurgi and shrugged. "Of course, you remember this was not my idea. We walked up and down Arndt Street, knocking on doors, and asked if anyone recognized this dog. Nobody did."

Papa shoved his chair back and strolled toward the steps. "Yurgi, you know the dog's name is not really Goldy, but for now, to make it easy, let's call her that."

Yurgi grinned and took one step. Goldy stepped up, too, and posed with her front feet by Yurgi.

Papa sat on the top step and scratched the dog's ears. "Maybe she ran far away from her home." Papa turned to Yurgi. "Just because we can't find her owner on Arndt Street doesn't mean that a little boy somewhere is not crying for his dog. We will put signs around town to see if we can find Goldy's owner."

Papa twisted around to glance at Taty. She nodded. Papa touched Yurgi's shoulders and stared into his eyes. "For now, we will give Goldy a warm place to sleep and some food but only until her real owner arrives."

"Did you hear that, Goldy?" Yurgi patted her back. "You get to stay with me."

"For now." Papa stood.

"For now," Yurgi repeated.

"But a house is no place for an animal," Papa said. "Goldy is probably a hunting dog, and she will be quite comfortable in our shed tonight."

We set about to make Goldy happy. Taty gathered some old quilts for a warm bed in the straw pile. Alya filled a flat dish with water while I cooked Goldy a bowl of oatmeal. I stirred it until it cooled then sprinkled bits of ham on top. She lapped up her water and gobbled her supper, there by the backdoor.

Then Papa, Yurgi, and I led Goldy to the shed. Yurgi held the lantern while I spread out the quilts and patted her new bed, signaling that it was hers. Goldy understood and crept onto it, turned in two circles, and lay down, resting her nose on her front paws.

Yurgi sat on the edge of Goldy's bed. "I think she's smiling." He held her head with both hands. "Will you be happy here?"

In answer, Goldy closed her eyes. We tiptoed out and latched the shed door. As we walked back to the house, a few snowflakes fell.

Papa shivered. "I can never get used to an October snowfall. Thank goodness Goldy is in a warm dry place. I wish we knew where Jimmy is."

Marty and Roy stepped out from the shadows by the backdoor. "So do we," she said. "We are not giving up on finding Jimmy, but we're giving up on it tonight. He is probably holed up someplace. It will be impossible to find him until daybreak."

Roy touched Papa's arm. "Please sir, could Marty stay here?"

CHAPTER 27

Tuesday

Marty slept in Yurgi's bed. Yurgi slept on the bed-couch in the living room and the new, kinder Eddy took Roy to his house where Eddy said the spare bedroom could use a guest again.

Morning arrived too early. "Wake up, Lis." Papa brushed my hair back. "It's time to get ready for work at Infant Socks."

"I'm so tired, Papa. Can't I sleep a few more minutes?"

"Sorry, Lis. We need to do the chores for Taty before we head to work. Her cut hand was throbbing all night. I want to let her sleep and heal."

"Me too." I sighed and lifted the quilts on my side of the bed.

"Can you take care of feeding Goldy?"

"I'll be right there," I whispered and glanced at Alya and Marty, both unmoved and breathing deeply.

In the kitchen, Papa pumped water into the bucket for the chickens and Gertrude, our pig, and headed out to the chicken coop and pig pen.

Papa had already added wood to the stove. I pumped our big kettle half full of water and slid it onto the hot stove to make oatmeal for the family. While it heated, I brought a little pan of water to boiling for Goldy's oatmeal breakfast. When the oatmeal was soft, I added a little ham again and cooled the mixture with a dribble of milk.

Balancing Goldy's bowl of oatmeal and her refilled water dish, I took careful steps down. Papa had left the inside door open, so I nudged the storm door with my hip and slipped out. The cold air froze my nostrils, and I gasped.

"Snow," I mumbled. "I forgot it was snowing last night." About two inches of white stuff covered our grass and clung to the apple tree branches. I shuffled to the shed, careful to not spill anything. Outside the door, I skidded to a stop, and the water sloshed over my hand. The door hung open an inch.

"Papa," I yelled. "Did you unlatch the shed door?"

He was sliding a wire ring over the chicken pen gate and spun around. "No, Lis, I haven't been near the shed this morning."

I kicked the door open with my foot. Goldy glanced up from her bed and sniffed. Still balancing her breakfast, I went to her, placed her breakfast down, and knelt in front of her. "Did you open the door, girl?" Goldy cocked her head sideways, stretched to stand up, and devoured her breakfast in two slurps.

Papa called from outside. "Looks like Goldy had a visitor during the night. Come see these footprints."

He crossed his arms, waiting for me to examine the snow. I raised both eyebrows. "I'd say they belong to a ten-year-old boy, wouldn't you?"

"Let's go tell Marty."

I shook her awake. "I have good news," I whispered. "Come with me."

She rubbed her eyes, wrapped a shawl around her shoulders, and staggered into the kitchen, still half asleep. "Did you find Jimmy?" She slid into a chair and leaned forward. "You won't find him if he doesn't want to be found."

I stood by the stove eating a bowl of oatmeal. Before pushing the kettle to the warming area, I whisked the oatmeal in the kettle and put a lid on it.

Papa sat down next to Marty. "That makes our news even better. Somebody left tracks outside the shed and probably spent the night inside with Goldy. If Jimmy is as good at hiding as you say, he made a careless mistake, or he wants to be found."

"It could be that Jimmy wants to be found. Maybe he even realizes that his stubborn anger got him into trouble again." Marty chewed on her bottom lip. "Or it could be a mistake. He has a soft heart when there's a dog involved. Every time he and Pa argued, Jimmy would storm out to the barn and cry into our old mutt's fur. That old mutt just let him cry his heart out."

Papa drummed his fingers on the table. "Well, either way, I think Goldy is the bait to catching Jimmy. Let's go on with life as if we don't have a clue. Perhaps you and Roy can even walk through a couple of hobo jungles during the day, searching."

Papa slid his chair back. "Please remind Yurgi to give Goldy a walk around our yard and help Taty get the little ones off to school."

Marty blinked back tears. "I will. Thank you for everything."

I lifted my hand. "Oh, and remind Yurgi not to tell anyone about Eddy and Miss Meuschlin."

Papa's eyes got big. "That's a story for another day." He held out his arm for me. "May I escort you to your first day at Infant Socks?"

My feet turned to cement blocks. Why had I volunteered to fill in for Taty? With dread, I dragged myself along with Papa.

CHAPTER 28

"How old are you, girl?" Mr. Luczak glared down his nose at me, peering between his wire-rimmed glasses and his bushy eyebrows.

I cowered against the wall in his office, staring at my sturdy brown shoes. "A-a-almost fifteen, sir."

"Look at me when I'm talking to you."

"Y-y-yess, sir." Unable to look at him, I focused on a fly on the wall above his head.

"Did you know that it's against the law to hire a girl before she's seventeen?" Mr. Luczak twisted around to see what I was staring at, then he turned to me. "I'm not sure what our policy is for substitute workers, but until I talk to Mr. Hanisch, the plant manager, I'm going to put you out on the floor in Taty's position. We have too many orders coming in to leave her post vacant."

"Thank you, Mr. Luczak. I'll try my b-b-best."

"Well, off with you then. Your father is hovering outside my door. He'll show you where to go."

Papa led me through the second floor where women and girls were standing and chatting. A friendly buzz filled the air. Papa pointed to a chair in a row of long worktables. Each chair had a cutting contraption on the table in front of it. "That's where you'll snip half socks from the big roll coming from production. I have to get to my workroom now." I sat down, and he rushed off as a bell clanged.

Women and girls scooted into their chairs. The buzz of conversation stopped just as Mr. Luczak strolled from his office and scanned the room.

"I'm Doris," an older lady sitting on my right whispered. "For now, start cutting like this." She picked up a long tube of sock tops from a basket at her feet and quickly snipped the tiny threads around the first one, separating it from the long strand of sock tops. "It's not difficult work, just tedious. When Mr. Luczak heads back into his office, I'll help you more."

Mr. Luczak glanced from one table to the next then paced up and down each aisle until he came to me. I fumbled with my first sock top but tried to follow Doris's hasty instructions. He rocked back and forth, heels to toes, heels to toes, and stared at me. My hands shook, but I worked the sock top through the cutter with a sigh of relief.

"Not bad for you first attempt." Mr. Luczak strolled away with is hands clasped behind his back.

"Not bad for your first attempt," the girl on my left whispered in a mocking voice. I glanced at her as I started my second cutting. She was a little older than me. A frown puckered her eyebrows.

"Thanks," I said.

"That wasn't a compliment, missy. I'm just wondering how you can waltz in here and get the boss's praise so quickly."

Doris leaned forward to stare past me. "Betsy, stop being a self-centered brat. Lis, here, needs our help."

Mr. Luczak spun around and headed in our direction. He stopped in front of me again. "There's too much talking going on here. Is everything alright?" His stare went from Betsy to me to Doris.

I ducked my head to finish cutting my second sock top. Doris got back to work, too, but Betsy met his stare, "Yes, sir, just helping the new girl get started."

He raised one eyebrow. "Being helpful would be a new role for you, Betsy. For now, I'd like Doris to take over the training of Lis. Now all of you get to work."

"I can tell you're going to be trouble here." Betsy knocked my elbow with hers, and my hand slip.

"Oh, no, you made me cut the wrong thread." I turned to Doris. "What happens now?"

"Your pay will be docked by a penny, dear." Doris glared at Betsy. "Any more tricks like that, Betsy, and I'm reporting you to Mr. Luczak."

I worked faster as the day continued. I had twenty-two completed sock tops in my basket when the bell clanged again.

"It's 10 a.m." Doris pushed her chair back, stood, and stretched. "We have fifteen minutes to use the bathroom and eat our sandwiches." She peeked into my basket. "Looks like you're almost to your first twenty-four."

I straightened my aching back. "If I counted right, I'm at twenty-one. Three more, and I'll be ready for my next basketful."

"Come with me." Doris took my arm. "I'll show you the lunchroom and bathroom." As we walked, I explained how I was filling in for Taty.

In a few minutes, the warning bell sounded. "We better hurry back to our worktables," Doris said. "If we're not working when the next bell sounds, another penny will be subtracted from our pay."

Betsy was hunched over, already at work. She didn't glance at me as I sat down and pulled out my basket of completed sock tops. I counted them again. "Nineteen. Hey, I'm missing two sock tops. Does anyone know where they are?"

"I was in the bathroom. I didn't see anyone." Betsy smirked but kept her head down.

CHAPTER 29

When the one o'clock bell clanged, I hurried outside, feeling pretty proud of myself. Even with two of my sock tops mysteriously disappearing, I still managed to cut four dozen. Papa and Heinrich were leaning on Heinrich's car. The bright sun reflected off the hood. All evidence of snow was gone.

"Oh, there you are," Papa called. "Heinrich offered to give you a ride to school every day this week."

I ran up and hugged Heinrich. "Thank you! You're my hero."

"Ahem." Papa stepped up. "I'm the one who arranged it."

"Then you get a hug too.

Betsy strolled by. "Quite a cozy welcoming committee, Lis." She flipped her messy black hair and kept going.

"Isn't that the girl who sits beside you?" Papa asked. "Is she upset about something?"

"She's upset about everything." I shrugged. "Her eyebrows were knit together in a frown from the moment I sat down."

I paused, waiting for Papa to get my word joke. He laughed and mussed my hair.

I giggled, pleased, but I tapped on his chest. "And I think she stole two of my sock tops. Luckily, I still completed forty-eight, so my pay won't be docked another penny."

"It's a tough world at Infant Socks." Heinrich winked and opened the door for me. "Just think how tough it would be if you worked at Adult Socks."

"Heinrich, sometimes you're almost funny." Papa shut my door and nudged Heinrich toward his. "Lis could have walked halfway to school by now. Get going." Papa stepped back and waved as Heinrich shifted into gear.

I sank into the seat, easing my back straight. "Why aren't you at work this week?"

"I don't have to work this week. That's the bad part. With the Depression sweeping across our country, fewer products are being shipped anywhere, so the trains are reducing their schedules."

"What's the good part?"

"Actually, there are two good parts. I get to drive a pretty young lady to school all week." He glanced back and wiggled his eyebrows. "And next week I will work again. One week on. One week off." Heinrich pulled up to the curb. "Here we are."

I pushed the car door open. My arms were heavy. My back ached, and I was exhausted from the stress of my first day at work. "Am I glad that I only have this schedule for one week. I'm going to need a weeklong nap to catch up."

"That's not going to happen." Heinrich chuckled. "You have two hobos to keep warm, one boy hobo to find, a lost dog to feed, and, and, and, there must be something more. There always is with you."

I laughed and shut the door. "Thank you," I yelled through the window.

As Heinrich sped toward Main Street, Miss Meuschlin called from the door of St. Peters and ran down the sidewalk toward me. "I've been watching for you," she said, breathless. "Yurgi told me you'd be here about now."

"What's wrong with Yurgi?"

"Nothing's wrong with Yurgi."

I quit holding my breath. "Who's with your classroom, Miss Meuschlin? It's not like you to leave your students unattended."

"They're fine. Don't worry about them, Lis. It's Eddy we should worry about. He's missing."

"Missing?"

"Not exactly missing, as far as I know, but he didn't keep his appointment with me." She blushed and sputtered. "Well, it wasn't exactly an appointment, but he said he was stopping in at noon today."

She wrung her hands. "You and Eddy have a special bond. Do you know anything? I'm afraid something terrible has happened to him." She swiped at a tear. "He's always on time. I'm sure he would have gotten a message to me if he had to cancel."

"I wonder if he took Roy somewhere," I thought aloud. "He's the hobo that Eddy took home last night."

Miss Meuschlin gasped and wrung her hands more. "Did you say Eddy invited a hobo named Roy to his house last night? What if he kidnapped Eddy and is holding him for ransom? You know Eddy has money."

I squeezed my eyes shut for a second. As Heinrich predicted, something more was happening.

CHAPTER 30

I longed to hurry into WLA for my last two classes of the day. At least that would have given me a head start on the stack of homework I'd be facing tonight. Max and Hildy had promised to collect the assignments for me and put all my books into a satchel.

I glanced at the doors, then I looked at Miss Meuschlin. I knew what I wanted to do. I also knew what I should do. Miss Meuschlin's eyes were red and brimming with tears. I made my decision.

I hugged her. "I'm sure we can sort this out after school. We would have heard if anything bad happened to Eddy. For now, it's important that you return to your classroom." I led Miss Meuschlin back to St. Peter's and up the steps toward her first and second grade classroom.

"You're right, Lis. Eddy would want me to do the right thing. I've always been responsible. First I cared for my sick mother, then after she passed away, I got my teaching degree. Maybe that's why I never had a boyfriend. I was too responsible. Now, I've grown so fond of Eddy that I'm afraid I'll lose him."

"So Yurgi was right." I stopped on the top step and took hold of her hands. "You love Eddy."

She nodded. "But it's our secret for now."

"Don't worry. I gave Yurgi strict instructions to keep quiet."

"He adores you, Lis. I know he'll keep our secret, even though it will be a struggle for him to not talk." We laughed together.

"Why don't you walk home with us after school? Taty has been there all day and will know what's going on."

"That's a good plan, Lis. Thanks for calming me down." She took a deep breath.

Outside her room, Miss Meuschlin dabbed her eyes with her handkerchief and ran her fingers through her hair. All was quiet. I should have known better than to have doubted that everything was fine. Miss Meuschlin loved her students, but she was strict with them. Any disobedience was punished. All of us quickly learned to follow the rules.

"Meet us on the sidewalk outside," I said, trying to not disturb the students and tore down the steps. Maybe I could still make it to my last class.

After school, Max, Hildy, and I waited outside St. Peter's school. Yurgi burst through the doors first. "Lis, did you know Miss Meuschlin is walking home with us? I'm really excited to show her my new dog, Goldy."

"Goldy is not your dog."

"She will be. You'll see." Yurgi's grin filled his face.

Alya and Miss Meuschlin pushed the heavy door open and held hands as they stepped down. Alya grabbed my hand with her free one. "I've been telling her about Marty, Roy, and Jimmy."

"You had a busy few days." She brushed my cheek with her hand. "No wonder your eyes are red."

"Ja, I am tired, tired all over. I don't think Alya had time to tell you everything. I'm not even sure I can remember everything."

Max stepped in front of Alya and Miss Meuschlin. "Lis, please, let me carry your books home for you." He pried the book satchel from my grip and led the way down the sidewalk.

"Thanks, Max. My hands and arms could use a rest."

Yurgi ran to keep up with him. Hildy grabbed my free hand. The four of us swung our arms together and strolled down the sidewalk. I glanced at Miss Meuschlin. She was flushed from the exercise, but a small smile played over her face.

"Are you better?" I asked.

"Yes, thanks to you."

At our front steps, Yurgi tugged on Miss Meuschlin's arm. "Come with me to the shed. I'm sure Goldy was missing me all day." Yurgi pumped his free arm and dragged her along. She glanced back, a lopsided grin on her face.

Max presented my books to me with a somber nod. "Here you go, Lis. Would you like me to stop in a little later to see if you have any questions?"

"Really, Max?" Hildy sputtered.

I interrupted before an argument started. "Thanks, Max, for all your kindness, but I think I'll be fine. Where would I be without both of you?"

They continued north on Brooke Street while Alya and I stepped into the living room and headed for the kitchen. "Mama, we're home," Alya called.

The backdoor slammed open and shut. Yurgi charged into the kitchen with Miss Meuschlin trailing behind. "Mama, where is Goldy? She's gone."

CHAPTER 31

Taty was standing at the stove, stirring cornmeal mush with her good hand. She spun toward us, then toward Yurgi and Miss Meuschlin. "Well, hello everyone. Welcome, Miss Meuschlin. What a pleasant surprise."

Yurgi ran up to Taty and pulled her down to face him. "Mama, please, tell me that Goldy is alright."

Taty slid the pan of mush back to the warming space and sat down, pulling Yurgi onto her lap. "Goldy is just fine. She's helping Roy, Marty, and Eddy search for Jimmy."

Miss Meuschlin plopped down in the next chair. She pressed her hand to her cheek. "Really? Eddy skipped work to help find the runaway boy? Isn't he sweet?"

Taty's eyes twinkled. "Marty dressed in your hobo clothes, Lis, and I found some old rags from Papa for Roy, but Eddy couldn't decide what to wear. He had brought a bag of clothes along, but no matter what he put on, he always looked nice."

Miss Meuschlin interrupted Taty's story again. "He does always look nice, doesn't he?"

Taty's eyes twinkled a little more before she continued. "Then Roy said, 'I can handle this.' He smeared some dirt on Eddy's face and clothes, tore the sleeve of his jacket, and smashed his hat."

Taty put her hand over her mouth, stifling a giggle. "You should have seen the shocked look on Eddy's face when he peeked into my hand mirror. I'm a little surprised that they're not back. They left late morning."

Yurgi wiggled around and patted Taty's cheek. "I like your story, Mama, but how will Goldy help them find Jimmy?"

"She's a hunting dog," Taty said. "She can follow his smell. His scent."

I hit my head with the palm of my hand. "Of course she can. Goldy is a hunting dog. Why didn't I think of that?"

Taty grinned at me. "It could be that you were working for me at Infant Socks."

"Or it could be you were calming me down in the school yard." Miss Meuschlin patted my hand and laughed.

"But Goldy doesn't know Jimmy, does she?" Yurgi frowned. "How can she follow his scent?"

I knelt down in front of Yurgi. "This morning Papa and I found little shoeprints in the snow outside the shed. We think Jimmy slept there with Goldy last night. Here we were worried about

Jimmy, and he was curled up with Goldy, snoring away under Mama's warm quilt."

"That's right," Taty said. "You and Papa told Marty what you discovered this morning, but none of us knew it. When Roy and Eddy came over after breakfast, Marty mentioned the footprints. Those two men's eyes got big, and they jumped up with excitement."

Taty leaned back. "I already told you the rest."

I smiled at Taty. "That's the longest story you've ever told. Papa usually tells the long ones. Isn't he home?"

"He came home after work, ate some lunch, and headed out the front door. He said he had to discuss some business with Heinrich." Taty smiled at me and gave Yurgi a hug. "When those two get together, they tease each other like little boys. I hope they aren't getting into any mischief."

A puzzled frown filled Yurgi's face. "Papa is too big to get into mischief, isn't he?"

CHAPTER 32

———•—•—•—•—•———

The front door rattled open. "Hellooo," Heinrich called.

"We're home." Papa followed Heinrich into the kitchen, and they plopped down on chairs. "We put up a few signs around town, describing Goldy and asking anyone who knows her owner to contact us."

Yurgi raced to Papa and pulled on his sleeve. "No, Papa, Goldy is my dog. I'm her owner." Yurgi's bottom lip stuck out. "Mama was right. You were up to mischief."

Papa glanced at Taty. "Mischief?"

She grinned. "Good mischief."

Papa put his arm around Yurgi and touched his pouting lip. "We have to try to find Goldy's real owner. It's the right thing to do."

Yurgi leaned into Papa. "I will be very sad to lose Goldy."

"I know," Papa said. "But there's a good chance Goldy has been abandoned. In this Depression, parents don't even have enough food to feed their own children. They have nothing left to feed a dog, so they take their dogs into the country and leave them there, hoping somebody will take them in."

"Do you think somebody left Goldy in the country? And that nobody wants her?" Yurgi's voice rose higher with each question. "And that we can take her in?"

Papa sighed. "We'll see. I'm still worried about having enough food for all of us. Taty and I are blessed to have good jobs, but what if we lose them tomorrow? How can we feed a big dog like Goldy?"

Quiet Alya stared up at Papa. "God says to not worry. You know that, Papa."

He studied her upturned face. "Ja, I do. Thanks for reminding me. I bet you can even recite the Bible passage."

Alya took a deep breath. "Matthew 6:34, 'Do not worry about tomorrow, for tomorrow will care for itself. Each day has enough trouble of its own.'"

I looked from Papa to Alya. "Well, that's not very encouraging. Why does every day have to have trouble?"

Heinrich slapped his knee. "Lis, I'm with you. I'd like a day without trouble once in awhile."

Papa shook his head. "When it comes to mischief, I'd say we have to watch out for you two. May I remind you that God also says that he will take care of our needs, like food and clothing, and that we shouldn't worry."

"I'll try not to worry, Papa," Yurgi said. "I know we'll always have enough food for Goldy because God said."

Heinrich slapped his knee again. "Taty and Pavel, your children are so entertaining."

Marty peeked in the backdoor. "May we come in?"

Yurgi dashed to the top step. "Come in. Come in. Did Goldy find Jimmy?" He peeked around Marty, Roy, and Eddy as they came up the steps. "Where is Goldy?"

"Yurgi, give them a chance to get into the house." I pulled up three chairs for them.

"Thanks, Lis." Eddy sat down beside Miss Meuschlin and scooted his chair closer. He patted her hand. "I'm sorry I didn't keep our appointment at noon. I felt this was a more pressing matter and knew you'd understand."

She squeezed his hand before he pulled it back. "I do."

Yurgi tapped his foot. "Is this enough time, Lis?"

Marty answered. "Yes, Yurgi, thanks for giving us a minute to catch our breath. We took Goldy on a stroll through the hobo jungle near here and also near Five Corners. While the hobos flocked to pet Goldy, nobody had seen Jimmy."

Eddy leaned forward. "I knew of another hobo jungle between the railroad tracks and Lake Winnebago. We all hopped in my automobile and took Goldy up there to sniff around. Goldy perked up and tugged on her rope."

Marty closed her eyes. "I was holding onto Goldy's rope, but not as tightly as I should have been. She yanked it from my hands and raced away. We lost sight of her in the trees and reeds along the lake."

"We searched and called for an hour and found nothing," Eddy said.

I rested my chin on my hands. "This is enough trouble for today."

The front door banged open. "Lis!" Max called.

"We have news." Hildy burst into the kitchen.

Heinrich glanced at me. "Double trouble," he muttered.

CHAPTER 33

Max trailed in behind her. Hildy took a deep breath. "When we arrived at Grandma's house, she was just getting home from taking cookies to a sick lady on Scott Street." Hildy set a plateful of cookies on our table. "Here. She sent some for all of you too."

"Get to the point." Max glared at her.

She gave him a little shove. "I am getting there."

"Let me handle this." Max stepped forward. "Yurgi was telling me about his new dog Goldy."

"Goldy is not his dog." I shook my head at Yurgi.

Yurgi stomped his foot. "She will be."

Heinrich stared at the ceiling. "See what I mean?"

"This is serious." Max lowered his voice. "Grandma saw a gold-colored dog racing west on Scott Street. The dog had a rope dragging behind. Is Goldy still in the shed?"

"No, she ran away." Yurgi covered his eyes with his hands and sobbed.

"Let's think this through." Papa glanced at Heinrich. "You're a hunter. What if Goldy found Jimmy's scent and followed it into the trees?"

Heinrich crossed his arms. "A good hunting dog could do that."

"And what if Jimmy had already left the area?" Papa asked. "Could Goldy follow his trail?"

Heinrich nodded.

Marty tapped the table. "If I were Jimmy, I'd know you'd be searching hobo jungles near here. And if I were Jimmy, I'd maybe stop at that hobo jungle for directions, but I'd be on my way before a search party arrived."

"Where could he be headed?" Eddy asked. "Is there another hobo jungle on the west side of town?"

Roy glanced at Marty. "Not west, but he was probably planning on turning north. We had talked about going to the hobo jungle in North Fond du Lac near the train yard and hopping a train there."

For a moment, nobody spoke. Heinrich glanced at Eddy, and they jumped up at the same time. "Let's take our automobiles," Eddy said. Heinrich nodded.

"Will all of us fit?" I asked.

"I don't think we'll have that trouble today." Papa winked at me.

"A day of trouble?" I shook my head at his word joke.

All of us—Papa, Taty, Yurgi, Alya, Max, Hildy, Eddy, Miss Meuschlin, Heinrich, Roy, Marty, and I—raced to the front door and ran to the two automobiles.

Papa opened the backdoor of Heinrich's automobile and boosted the little ones into the backseat. He held Taty's hand as she slid in too. Then I jumped in and he ran around to the front door while Heinrich started the car and shifted into gear. The others had piled into Eddy's automobile and were already roaring north on Brooke Street.

"Hurry, Heinrich." Yurgi stood on the floor with his head between Heinrich and Papa. "We have to find them first. Goldy and Jimmy will come to me because I'm their friend."

Both automobiles turned left on Scott Street and then right on the road toward North Fond du Lac. We headed for the train yard and the hobo jungle that was scattered beyond it.

This hobo jungle was the biggest in the area. Hobos could easily jump on and off trains here when they switched cars or dropped off shipments.

"What if Jimmy is already on a train?" I asked. "We'll never find him."

"What if he takes Goldy with him?" Yurgi sniffled. "I will have lost two friends at once."

The sun had set, but the red and gold-streaked sky gave us enough light to still see. We pulled up beside Eddy, already parked on the edge of the train yard. Papa said, "Let's not talk about 'what ifs' right now. Scan the area for any movement. Look in the train yard and around the edges."

We all squinted into the dusk, hoping and praying we weren't too late.

"What's happening over there?" I pointed to a sidetrack. A train was rolling backward.

"Oh, that's just a train dropping off empty boxcars," Heinrich said.

I stared harder. "I don't mean the train, but the movement beside it or below it. I can't tell. I think there are people."

At the same time, Marty flung open the backdoor of Eddy's automobile and screamed. "It's Jimmy with Goldy! And a stranger." She dashed across the train yard. "Jimmy, get away from that train! It's moving!"

Yurgi and I raced after Marty and skidded to a halt beside her, several feet from the moving train. Jimmy was sprawled on the ground with one of his legs in a crooked angle, his foot against the track. The boxcars rumbled above him. His eyes were big with fright as the strange man lunged forward, swinging a big stick. Goldy never took her eyes off the man. She snarled and crouched, ready to pounce.

CHAPTER 34

"Marty, help me!" Jimmy shouted. "I'm stuck! That big engine is getting close." He waved one arm frantically.

I glanced down the tracks. The rods turning the wheels of the engine dipped low, low enough to mangle Jimmy's leg. As the engine, belching steam, crept closer, boxcars rolled above him. Jimmy leaned on one elbow and glared at the man. "Mister, quit scaring my dog."

The rest of our search party staggered up, panting. Heinrich pointed. "That's Walter, the train yard supervisor."

Walter glared at Jimmy. "Well, how am I going to release your foot if that mutt won't even let me get near you?"

Heinrich grabbed Walter's shoulder. "Let me handle it!"

Walter spun around, his tense shoulders sagging. "Heinrich, yes. I'm getting nowhere. What a little spitfire brat and vicious mutt."

"First, drop the stick." Heinrich frowned. "Now back up. You're scaring the dog." Walter obeyed.

Yurgi called. "Hello, girl. Don't be afraid."

Goldy swiveled her head toward Yurgi. Her tail wagged. Her whole body wiggled with happiness. Everyone else stood back, breathless.

"Take slow steps to Goldy." I nudged Yurgi.

He crept forward, one hand held open. "Everything is fine now, Goldy. I'm here." She stepped toward Yurgi and nuzzled his hand. As he petted her head, she leaned against him.

"Yurgi, grip the rope around Goldy's neck and keep petting her," Heinrich said. "We need to free Jimmy's foot and must keep Goldy out of the way." Heinrich turned around. "See how his foot is wedged between the rail and the crosstie? Whom will Goldy trust with Jimmy?"

"Me." I stepped forward. "She'll trust me."

I crept around Goldy, running my hand over her head, then dropped to my knees and crawled toward Jimmy. The train was still backing up above us, the steel wheels of the boxcars clicking only inches from Jimmy's foot. Still, there was enough room for me to squat down and wiggle his leg.

"Ow! That hurts." Jimmy kicked me back with his other leg. I landed hard on my bottom.

"Jimmy," Marty yelled, "control your anger. Lis is trying to help you."

"Sorry, Lis." Jimmy squirmed and groaned. "It hurt so much I just kicked."

"I know." I blinked back tears and crawled up again. When I untied his shoe, I still couldn't coax his foot out. I wiggled his ankle, careful to not hurt Jimmy more. But the roar of the engine was deafening. I glanced over my shoulder. Horror shook me. The backing engine was almost upon us. Steam spewed from under it. The rods turning the wheels would crush Jimmy's leg.

Ignoring his screams of pain, I yanked his foot free and dragged him away from the tracks. I threw myself over him, shielding him from the dust and steam and tucked my head into his chest just as the seething engine rolled above us and farther down the track.

When the air settled, I opened my eyes. Jimmy's face was only inches away. His eyes stared into mine.

"You saved my life," he whispered.

I rolled off him and squeezed his hand. "Your life is worth saving."

CHAPTER 35

As the train backed farther down, clearing the tracks beside us, our friends and family swooped in. Marty collapsed over Jimmy, sobbing and holding him tight. Miss Meuschlin cried into Eddy's raggedy hobo jacket. Papa kept one arm around Taty, holding her up. Heinrich pounded Roy on his back, then Roy pounded Heinrich's. Max and Hildy stood arm in arm, for once speechless. And Goldy, dragging Yurgi along, bounded up to us and licked Jimmy's face and then mine. She jumped up and gave Yurgi a slobbery kiss too.

Squatting above Jimmy, Marty frowned. "You have a lot of explaining to do, young man."

Jimmy glanced at me, his eyes big and sad. I lifted one eyebrow and said to Marty, "We'll have time for that later."

Everyone was exchanging stories and not paying attention to us. "Hey, we're still down here." I was flat on my back in the dirt. Jimmy was wedged between Marty and me, also lying in the dirt. "Could someone help us get up?"

They fluttered over. Max got to me first, reached out his hand, and pulled me to my feet. He kept hold of my hand, his face beaming. "That was some rescue." He forgot to lower his voice.

"Thanks, Max." I brushed dust from my hands. "And thanks for what you did. We'd never have found Jimmy if not for you and Hildy."

The twins grinned at each other.

Marty grabbed Jimmy under his arms and tugged. "I'm sorry I scolded you. I was so scared I was going to lose you."

"Stop! Stop!" Jimmy bent forward in pain. "Ow! You're hurting me."

Marty lowered him down to the ground again. Roy stooped to examine his leg. He grimaced. "I'm not a doctor, but I'm pretty sure it's broken. Really broken."

The group gawked. Jimmy's right leg bent out at an ugly angle between his knee and ankle.

Papa knelt over Jimmy. "That's broken for sure. We have to get him to a doctor, but let's brace his leg first. We need something straight and strong." Papa glanced around.

"How about this stick?" The yard manager stooped down, picked it up, and handed it to Papa. "Maybe this is a better way to use it."

Papa grabbed the stick. "Thanks, sir! Now we also need to tie it onto Jimmy's leg."

"I have it." I ran to the track and wiggled Jimmy's shoe free. "Let's use his shoestring."

While Papa worked, Jimmy held Marty's hand. "I'm really sorry, Sis, that I put you through so much worry. Not just today, but always. Why do I get so upset and do stupid things?" Small tears leaked from the sides of his eyes.

"Shh, you don't have to talk now." Marty brushed his hair back.

"I wanted to get away from you and Roy. You have each other and shouldn't have to be bothered with me. I thought I could handle my own life."

"We want you in our lives." Marty swiped at a tear on her cheek.

A sob shook Jimmy's body. "I didn't think I deserved to be in a loving home like Pavel and Taty's. I was already feeling down when Yurgi announced that he was my friend. I couldn't stand it. Nobody ever cared for me. Why would they now? So I ran off, planning to hop a train and disappear."

"No poof this time." Yurgi glanced at me.

"My plan would have worked, except for this dog."

Goldy licked Jimmy's hand and wagged her tail.

"Last night, she followed me as I ran away. When my hat brushed off as I ducked under a branch, she picked it up. I kept running, cutting through yards and under bushes. Every time I stopped to rest, she sat down beside me and nuzzled my arm. We were taking a break when I saw an automobile come slowly up the street. I hid around the corner of the house to watch. Sure enough, there was Yurgi in the window, yelling at the dog. That dog was busy chasing a mouse, but as soon as she heard Yurgi, she tugged on my sleeve and took off after you."

"Why didn't you come out?" I asked. "We'd have been thrilled to take you home."

Another tear rolled down Jimmy's cheek. "Lis, I was too ashamed of myself for messing up again and too stubborn to admit I needed help. But when Goldy took off after your automobile, I had to follow her."

"Where were you when we tucked Goldy into the shed for the night?" I asked.

"Hiding behind it. I heard you call her Goldy and give her a good night pat. After the lights went out in the house, I snuck into the shed and curled up with her. Long before the sun came up, I hugged her goodbye and followed my plan to run faraway."

Papa sat back on his heels. "We're done here, son, but could you answer one more question? How is it you came to be stuck under a train?"

Jimmy reached up to pet Goldy's nose. "When I got to the train yard, I saw one train moving slowly. I took a running leap to jump into a boxcar, but something grabbed my jacket and yanked me back. It was Goldy, stopping me. As I tumbled down, Goldy jumped around, barking. When I tried to get up, I discovered my shoe was wedged between the track and the crossties. I didn't know what to do, but she did. She barked and barked until this man appeared." He nodded at the train yard manager.

"Thanks for your help, sir." Papa patted Goldy's head. "And thanks for your help too." Goldy wiggled all over, prancing between Yurgi and Jimmy. Papa gave me a long hug. "A really big thanks to you."

CHAPTER 36

Heinrich ran ahead to open his automobile doors. Roy and Papa lifted Jimmy between them, and Marty cradled his legs. Step by small step, they carried him. Roy scooted into the backseat first as Papa helped ease Jimmy in. He rested his head on Roy's lap. Jimmy winced as Roy pulled him a little further in so Papa could close the door. Marty, Papa, and Heinrich crowded into the front seat. With a wave and a toot of the horn, they sped off.

Eddy turned to the rest of us and counted. "One, two, three, four, five, six, seven, eight. I've never piled eight people into my automobile."

Goldy barked.

"Oh, sorry, Goldy. I didn't mean to forget you. That's eight people plus a dog. Miss Meuschlin, do you have any mathematical solution for this problem?"

Max stepped forward. "Allow me, sir. I love solving story problems."

"Really, Max." Hildy grabbed his arm and dragged him toward Eddy's automobile.

But Max wasn't done solving the problem. He stood outside the door, directing everyone with his lowered voice. "Eddy will need room to drive so we can't crowd the front seat. Let's put Miss Meuschlin close to Eddy." She slid in very close to him.

Max raised one eyebrow and glanced at me. I ignored him.

Next, I nudged Taty toward the open door. "We'll put you in the front seat, too, so that nobody bumps your sore hand."

Max studied the five people and one dog still standing. "The backseat will be trickier." He lifted his hands in defeat. "Let's just pile in, big ones first, and see what happens."

Max held Yurgi. I held Alya. Hildy put her feet on the seat so Goldy had the floor. It happened very well. We laughed all the way home.

We were still laughing as the top layer of people tumbled from the car. Max leaped out and offered his hand to me. "May I be of assistance?

"Well, thank you, kind sir," I said, taking his hand. He kept hold of my hand as we walked toward the porch.

Albert and John sat on the top step, glaring at us.

John stood and crossed his arms. "Where have you been? We've been waiting here for an hour."

"And why are you giggling with Max and holding his hand?" Albert jumped up and strolled closer.

"Did you know Goldy is gone?" John asked just as Hildy walked around the car with Goldy. "Oh, there she is. Why is she with Hildy?"

Albert stared at the automobile as everyone else climbed out. "I must say this is an odd, large group to go for a pleasure drive."

"Pleasure drive? We were taking care of the troubles of the day." I shook my head at Albert and John's crazy questions, then glanced at their confused frowns, and burst out laughing. Before long, everyone was giggling, except John and Albert.

"Why are we laughing?" Eddy leaned against the car, catching his breath.

"With relief, my dear." Miss Meuschlin leaned into him. "We were so frightened, and now our emotions are relaxing."

Albert tapped one foot. "Well, I don't find this funny. My natural curiosity is bouncing in my head. Lis, let's have the story."

Yurgi jumped up from petting Goldy. "Lis, please, please, let me tell the story."

Albert and John eased themselves onto the steps. "This could take a while," John said.

But it didn't. I interrupted Yurgi, then Max interrupted me, then Hildy took over. We sped through the story with everyone adding to it. By the time we were finished, Albert and John had slumped. Albert pinched his lips in a pout. "I can't believe you had all that excitement and didn't include us."

CHAPTER 37

Yurgi and Albert gave Goldy an extra big bowl of oatmeal and led her to the shed to her cozy bed. The rest of sat around the kitchen table, eating boiled eggs and homemade bread. We told and retold the details of our day.

Soon Yurgi burst through the backdoor. "Goldy is happy to be home again."

Albert latched the door and followed Yurgi up the steps. "I actually think she smiled at Yurgi before she closed her eyes."

"Goldy loves me best!" Yurgi announced. "I'm her person, right Lis?"

I pulled him into a hug. "Probably. We'll see."

"Well, friends, who needs a ride?" Eddy scooted his chair back, and everyone but John got up to leave.

"Thanks, Eddy," John said, "but I think I'll wait here for a while. Maybe I can say something to help Jimmy."

＋ ＋ ＋ ＋ ＋

Two hours later, Taty was resting in her bedroom, and I stood at the stove, frying slices of dried out cornmeal mush in lard. "We can pack these in our lunches tomorrow." I pushed the skillet back to cool and collapsed onto a chair. The excitement of the day made me feel like a limp dumpling.

Yurgi slid onto my lap and yawned. "Where is Papa? We've been waiting forever."

I pulled Yurgi closer. "Only a couple hours. Jimmy's leg was badly broken. It might take the doctor a long time to fix it. You and Alya may wait up for a few minutes yet, then it's off to bed for you."

John stood above Alya, listening to her memory work. He glanced at me. "Maybe a doctor can't fix it completely." John walked with a slight limp to sit beside Alya. "My foot will never be completely normal."

Yurgi's head drooped forward as I studied John. "Maybe our doctors are better here."

"I hope so for Jimmy's sake." John straightened his leg and flexed his crooked foot. "He's too young to go through life with a limp."

"So were you," I whispered.

The front door rattled, and Yurgi's eyes flew open. "They're here." He raced through the living room with John and me close behind.

"We're back." Heinrich held the door open as Roy and Papa carried Jimmy through and lowered him to the bed-couch. Marty followed, holding a pair of crutches.

"Is your leg fixed?" Yurgi crept up to Jimmy.

He pointed. "I reckon it looks straight again, but who can tell with that hard, white thing wrapped around it."

"That's called a cast," Papa said. "It will keep you from moving your leg until it's healed. I was proud of you, son. You didn't even scream when the doctor pulled it straight to set it."

"It was a horrible hurt." Jimmy shuddered. "I didn't scream on the outside, sir, but there were plenty of screams banging around in my head."

Heinrich and Papa laughed. Roy and Marty chuckled too. It was their turn for an emotional release.

+ + + + +

Marty set the crutches against the bed-couch and eased Jimmy back, placing a pillow under his head and another under the cast. "For now, you'll be sleeping here in the living room. Tomorrow I'll help you practice using your crutches. The doctor says you won't be walking on your leg for six weeks."

"Six weeks without walking?" Jimmy's eyebrows arched up. His mouth curved down.

John sat on the edge of the bed-couch. "Taking care of your broken leg now will be worth it." He held up his crooked foot. "I didn't get a doctor's care right away, and then it was too late to fix my foot. Please listen to your sister."

John nudged Jimmy's shoulder and got up. "Remember, I know what you're feeling right now. If you want to talk to someone, ask me."

"Let me give you a ride home, John," Heinrich said. "I best be getting back to sweet Rachel. I'm sure Frau Brunhild telephoned her with the news so she's not too worried."

Papa and I walked them to the door. Papa nudged Heinrich with his elbow.

"Six weeks without walking means six weeks without running too."

Heinrich's laughter followed him into the yard.

CHAPTER 38

Wednesday

My feet dragged as Papa and I walked to work the next morning. "I'm tired all over, Papa. How can I face Mr. Luczak's impatient tapping foot and Betsy's snippy voice?"

Papa linked his arm through one of mine. "I guess I'll have to recite a Bible passage or two since Alya isn't here. 'I can do all things through Christ who strengthens me.'" He lifted one eyebrow.

I didn't respond.

"Here's another one. 'Do not weary in doing good.'"

I stepped away from Papa. "I am weary, so weary."

He turned in front of me and touched my arm. "Think about this, Lis. You are a blessing to Taty, our whole family, and our old and newfound friends. God is using you to do good. Can you try your hardest?"

I gave a reluctant nod.

"Mr. Schallert, wait!" We spun around as Officer Kowalski hurried up. Papa stiffened a little. My whole body froze. Men in uniforms bothered Papa, too, but not as much as me.

"I've been waiting to catch you on your way to Infant Socks. Yesterday morning Max and Yurgi told me that you were helping the young hobos," Officer Kowalski said.

"We are," Papa said.

"As the Depression continues, we in government appreciate all that our citizens can do for the homeless." Officer Kowalski straightened his shoulders. "On the other hand, I want to do all I can to protect families like yours. That's why I'm here."

Papa frowned. "Do you think we're in danger?"

Officer Kowalski paused and chewed his upper lip. "Maybe. Yesterday afternoon as I was driving home from work, I noticed a man in a black-and-green plaid jacket hanging around the back of your property. Of course, I stopped and yelled out the window, but the man limped into the trees. By the time I parked, he had disappeared."

I grabbed Papa by the arm. "That must be Austin, the hobo who talked to Albert and me."

"You know him?" Officer Kowalski peered down.

"Not really. He was one of the hobos we served during Albert's Soup Saturday, and then he talked to us later about the young hobos. He didn't seem dangerous."

"Well, you never can tell what men will do in desperate times." Officer Kowalski straightened and glanced at Papa. "I'll stop by your house and remind Taty to keep your doors locked."

Papa shook the officer's hand and tugged my arm. "We better hurry, or we'll both have a day's worth of trouble before six o'clock."

"A day's worth of trouble? Papa, do you never quit teasing?"

Mr. Luczak stood by his office, scanning the work floor as I slid into my chair only seconds before the final bell clanged. "Whew!" I gave Doris a sideways glance. "That was close."

Doris picked up her first sock top. "That would have been another penny docked off your pay. Better be a little earlier tomorrow."

Betsy grabbed a sock top, too, but leaned toward me. "You work too slowly to deserve a full paycheck anyway."

Mr. Luczak strolled in our direction. I bit my bottom lip to keep from saying something nasty and grabbed my first sock top. I would show her.

Cutting sock tops apart was easier today. By the time the bell clanged for our break, I had twenty-seven in my basket. I counted to be sure and then pushed my basket farther under the table.

Doris stood and rolled her shoulders. "This is hard on my back, but I know I'm blessed to have this job when so many other people have lost theirs."

I stood and pushed my chair in. "Betsy, would you like to join us in the lunchroom today?"

She hunched over one more sock top. "No thanks." She didn't glance up. "I'm going to finish up a couple more."

I turned back several times as Doris and I walked away. Every time I peeked at Betsy, she was hard at work. But I didn't trust her.

"Doris, I finished twenty-seven sock tops already. I think somebody stole a few yesterday during our break, so I'm going to stand around the corner and keep watch."

"What about your break?" Doris stared at Betsy. "I'll hurry back and replace you for a couple minutes so that you can at least use the bathroom."

I grinned. "You're as sweet as Taty said."

Doris rushed off. I glanced back at my workstation just in time to see Betsy stoop down and pull sock tops from my basket.

"Thief!" I yelled, racing toward my chair. "Betsy is stealing my sock tops."

Mr. Luczak charged from his office door.

CHAPTER 39

Betsy slumped in a chair in Mr. Luczak's office. I sat in one next to her. Both of us faced his desk. She blew her nose into a crumpled handkerchief and then pressed it to her red eyes. I stared at a spider above Mr. Luczak's head. It had replaced the fly from yesterday. Had the spider eaten the fly?

Mr. Luczak's stern voice shook me from my drifting brain. "Stealing is a serious accusation." He stared at me without blinking. "Are you sure you didn't miscount, Lis? Betsy has been a faithful worker here for a few weeks. This is only your second day. Why should we believe your word over hers?"

My heart thumped in my chest. "I've tried my best, Mr. Luczak, and was pleased that I had finished more sock tops than yesterday. I know because I counted them when the break bell clanged."

"Why would I risk this job by stealing?" Betsy sniffled. "My pa left home to find work, and my ma hardly makes enough money doing people's laundry to feed the babies and me."

A soft knock sounded. Doris peeked around the door frame. "Excuse me, Mr. Luczak, I counted the sock tops in Lis's basket. She told me she had completed twenty-seven as we walked toward the lunchroom. Now her basket only has twenty-four." She held out my basket to him. "I thought you'd like to verify it."

"It's a lie," Betsy screamed. "You took three out. You two are trying to get me fired."

Doris slapped her hand to her chest. "Betsy, you have been self-centered and rude from the second you waltzed through the doors. Sometimes my sock top count came up short. Others have said the same, but we couldn't figure it out."

I glanced from Doris to Betsy.

Doris strolled in and faced Betsy, their noses inches apart. "You were the one stealing sock tops, weren't you? It's time you own up to what you've been doing."

Betsy eyes widened. "My family needs the money from this job more than either of you." Her voice cracked. "My pa isn't looking for another job. He walked out on us, said he was never coming back." Betsy hung her head. "I had to keep my count high so Mr. Luczak would think I was a good worker."

"Stealing is wrong." I glared at Betsy.

Doris patted my shoulder but stared at Betsy. "Don't you know the Seventh Commandment? 'Thou shalt not steal.' Does it say we should not steal unless we're afraid of losing our job? No. Does it say we should not steal unless we're hungry? No."

I rubbed my hand over my eyes. Something about this scene was familiar. This was like when we caught Jimmy stealing our chicken, Rosie. What had Papa said?

Suddenly, I remembered and blurted out, "Getting caught might have actually saved Betsy from bigger crimes." Everyone stared at me, frowning.

Just then Papa spoke from the doorway. "Excuse me, Mr. Luczak. Someone reported that there was noise coming from your office, so I came to check it out."

"Thanks, Pavel," Mr. Luczak shook his head. "We do have an incident here. Stealing is a crime that needs to be punished. I need to decide if I should fire Betsy."

Mr. Luczak faced me. "Lis, the crime was against you and against Doris and others too. What do you think?"

I glanced at Doris. Her face had softened. I turned to Betsy who was weeping into her soggy handkerchief.

My anger cooled. "Maybe she learned her lesson just by getting caught. Doris, can you think of a suitable punishment?"

Doris folded her hands on her stomach and stared at the spider. "Hmmm. Betsy has to pay for what she did to us. When the girls on the floor find out, they'll be furious, but now that I understand her situation, I don't think she should get fired. What if her pay is docked by five cents a day for the next month? Everyone on the floor should be satisfied with that."

"And what if Betsy apologizes to everyone she stole from?" I asked. "That should help too."

Mr. Luczak sighed and closed his eyes. I held my breath. With his eyes still shut, Mr. Luczak said, "Lis, can you recite 'What does this mean' from the Seventh Commandment?"

Now I closed my eyes. If only Alya were here to help me. I took a deep breath. "'We should fear and love God that we do not take our neighbor's money or property or get it by dishonest dealings, but help him to improve and protect his property and business.'"

When I opened my eyes, Mr. Luczak grinned at me. "Today you helped me and also your fellow workers to improve and protect our property and business."

Everyone smiled at me. Papa's smile meant the most.

CHAPTER 40

At one o'clock, Heinrich was outside Infant Socks, leaning on his automobile with his legs crossed. Papa and I swung out the factory doors at the same time. I paused to inhale the cool fall air, as if I were escaping a prison. I whispered, "Only three more days at Infant Socks."

"Why don't both of you jump in?" Heinrich called. "I have time to give Lis a ride to Winnebago Lutheran and you, Pavel, a ride home. Sweet Rachel has no extra errands for me today."

My afternoon at school was trouble free and, on our walk home, Max and Hildy didn't argue once. This had turned into a wonderful day.

Yurgi pranced ahead. "I'm going to say hello to Goldy." He dashed around the house toward the shed.

"Mama, we're home," Alya called, as the two of us stepped into the living room. Marty sat on the bed-couch with Jimmy. The house was quiet.

"Where are Papa and Taty?" I asked. "Didn't Heinrich drop off Papa?"

"Sure did," Jimmy said. "And Heinrich dropped in to say hello."

Marty slid off the bed-couch and walked toward us. "But they're not here now. I'm sorry, Lis. They took Taty to the doctor."

Jimmy scooted forward. "Don't worry none. She didn't break a leg or anything that bad."

"What happened?" I grabbed Marty by her hands. Alya clung to my arm.

"Taty was extra tired all day," Marty said. "She'd get up to do something and then sit down again with a sigh. I figured she was just exhausted from yesterday."

"But it was more than that, right?"

Marty nodded. "As soon as Pavel walked in the door, he glanced at Taty's flushed face and put his hand against her cheek. She was burning up with fever. Then Pavel studied Taty's arm above the bandage and held it up for Heinrich to see. There was a tiny red streak going partway up her arm."

"Infection." I sank to the floor. "That can be bad."

"Yes, it can be deadly." Marty sat down by Jimmy. Alya and I sat on the other side, quiet, waiting.

Yurgi ran past the window with Goldy galloping beside him. He pounded on the front door, then he popped in. "Goldy wants to come in and visit Jimmy. I promise I won't let go of her rope."

Jimmy's eyes lit up. "Please, Lis. I've been stuck in this boring room all day."

"Please, Lis," Yurgi chimed in. "Goldy has been stuck in that boring shed all day too. It will be good for everyone."

"Well, alright, just for a few minutes." I held the door open and petted Goldy as she trotted in. "But you keep a tight hold on her rope. We can't have Goldy chasing through the house and getting into mischief."

"Wahoo!" Jimmy pushed himself to the edge of the bed-couch. When Goldy saw him, her tail wagged and she jumped up beside him, towing Yurgi along. Jimmy brushed his hand down her head and patted her shoulder. "How are you today, girl?"

In answer, she nuzzled his hand.

Yurgi sat down and patted her other shoulder. "Do you want to be friends with Jimmy too?"

Jimmy sat up straighter. "She is already my friend. She followed me when I was running away the first time."

"Goldy wasn't your friend. She came to my house to find me." Yurgi leaned forward and glared at Jimmy. "I'm her person. I named her."

Yurgi turned his scowling face toward me. "Tell him, Lis. Goldy likes me best."

Jimmy crossed his arms. "Did she save you from jumping onto a train? No. She did me. Goldy also made sure I was safe until help arrived. She loves me best."

Both boys burst into tears, just as Papa and Heinrich helped Taty through the door.

"What's that dog doing in here?" Papa bellowed. "Dogs are meant to be outdoors."

I held my breath. The boys cried louder.

Papa pointed to the door. "Lis, now."

Jumping to obey, I tugged Goldy's rope. She followed willingly but paused at the door to glance back at Jimmy.

CHAPTER 41

In a few minutes, I dragged myself up the back steps, ashamed I had allowed Goldy into our house, breaking Papa's rule. He was waiting in the kitchen. "I'm sorry for yelling, Lis. I was upset you allowed a dog inside, but as I saw Goldy stare at Jimmy with such obvious love, I understood then that you were doing it for Jimmy. Will you forgive me for my impatience?"

"Of course, Papa." I hugged him.

He rested his hand on my shoulder. As we walked into the living room, he tipped his head toward Taty. "It's been a tough afternoon."

Taty had settled onto the bed-couch beside Jimmy and was leaning against the wall. When we approached, her eyes fluttered open. Jimmy grinned up at her. "I've been waiting to ask you, Taty. Did the doctor fix your inspection?"

Her tired face brightened. "Thanks for asking, Jimmy. You're showing us what a nice boy you can be."

Yurgi patted Taty's arm. "Isn't it called an infection, Mama?"

"Well, ja, but I knew what he meant."

Alya stepped closer. "You didn't answer Jimmy's question, Mama. Did the doctor fix you?"

Taty smiled at the little faces all turned to her. "Almost. The doctor checked my cut and found tiny threads still stuck in it. They were causing the infection, so he pulled them out and washed my thumb with hydrogen peroxide."

Papa pulled a bag from one pocket. "This is Epsom salt. She's supposed to soak her hand in warm Epsom salt water several times a day to pull out the infection."

From his other pocket, Papa lifted a jar. "And this is honey. After Taty soaks her hand, we are supposed to dab honey on her bandage and then wrap it around her thumb. Honey can help fight infection too." Papa's smile faded. "And that's about all we can do. It's up to God to help Taty's body heal. She needs lots of rest and good food."

"If she rests during this week, will that be good enough?" My shoulders sagged.Taty blinked back tears. "I'm sorry, Lis. The doctor says I have to rest for another week or two, and then we'll see how I am doing."

I slumped against the living room wall. Papa faced me. "Lis, please, don't be discouraged. We need you to work longer at Infant Socks. Hopefully, it won't be for long. I'll ask Mr. Luczak tomorrow if that is alright."

I stared at the satchel sitting on the floor, filled with books and papers for tonight's homework. I would stay up late to study. Tomorrow I would walk to Infant Socks early, hurry to school late, and come home to do homework again. When would it end? I slid to the floor, weighted down by the horrible circle of my days. I buried my face in my arms.

CHAPTER 42

Thursday

The next afternoon, Papa met me in the hall of Infant Socks. "Thanks for waiting for me, Papa."

He nodded and shuffled out the door, staring straight ahead.

"Hey, Pavel." Heinrich stood outside his car. "You want a ride home again?"

Papa kept staring. I tugged on his sleeve. "Papa, Heinrich is talking to you."

He focused on me and shook his head. "Oh, sorry, I was thinking." He flashed me a shaky smile and strolled up to Heinrich. "Sorry, old man. Thanks, anyway, but I need a walk to clear my head."

"Better be careful." Heinrich raised one eyebrow. "I don't give rides to people who call me old."

Papa hurried off, chuckling.

I slid into the front seat. "May I have a ride to school, young man?"

"Of course, my lady." We laughed together as Heinrich pulled out. "I stopped at your house this morning. I wanted to drop off an old brush for Goldy. She needs a good brushing, and there are two boys to oblige."

"I'm sure Goldy said thank you."

"Oh, and Rachel had baked fresh sweet rolls for your family. Yum. They were filled with raisins and sprinkled with cinnamon. You should have seen the smiles on Marty, Jimmy, and Roy's faces."

"Roy was there?" I shrugged. "I guess I didn't think about how he would spend his day. Where else could he go? Eddy's at work."

"He told me he came to help Jimmy with his crutches." Heinrich glanced at me and winked. "But Jimmy was swinging around the house quite well while Roy and Marty sat on the bed-couch, holding hands and laughing together."

"They're engaged, you know. But how can they get married? Papa says Marty and Jimmy may live with us for a while, and Eddy says he's happy to let Roy use his guest room."

My voice trailed off. We were trying to help the young hobos by feeding them and giving them warm rooms, but what did they really have? No money. No house. No job. No future. Nothing.

"Here we are." Heinrich nudged my arm. "Wake up! First your papa and now you. Did somebody name this National Daydreaming Day?"

"Sorry, Heinrich, I was thinking."

"Time to think about school. Now off with you." Heinrich swept his hand toward the door.

I giggled. "Thanks, Heinrich, for the ride and for always making me laugh."

"Oh, posh." His eyes twinkled. "I love making you laugh."

+ + + + +

During our walk home from school, Yurgi skipped ahead, then stopped and tapped his toe, waiting for us to catch up. "Why are you dragging along?" he whined before racing ahead.

"What's up with Yurgi?" Hildy asked.

"He's always jittery." Max shrugged.

"Really, Max?" Hildy sputtered. "He's just a little boy, full of energy."

Max glared at Hildy. "Well, I've never even seen Yurgi this energetic."

I grabbed Max's arm. "Really, Max?" Hildy giggled, but I continued, "Yurgi never slows down, but today he's extra excited because I told him Heinrich dropped off a brush for Goldy."

"He did? I want to help brush Goldy." Alya clapped her hands.

When we were a block from home, Yurgi ran sideways. "Lis, now may I run home? There are no more streets to cross."

"Me too?" Alya asked.

When I nodded, they raced down the sidewalk together but skidded to a halt below our front steps. Jimmy sat there, brushing Goldy.

As we approached, Yurgi stomped his foot. "It's not fair. Jimmy gets to spend all day with Goldy while I'm at school. Why did I ever think he was my friend? He's stealing my dog."

CHAPTER 43

I grabbed Yurgi's shoulder. "Jimmy is your friend, but he's a hurt little boy, and you need to be nice to him. Why can't you share Goldy?"

Alya glanced up at me with pleading eyes.

"And you must share Goldy with Alya too."

Yurgi hung his head.

"That's right," Papa said, opening the front door. "It's Yurgi and Alya's turn to brush Goldy now. Lis, could you and Jimmy come in please?"

Yurgi yanked the brush from Jimmy's hand and crossed his arms. Jimmy glared back but picked up his crutches and hopped up the steps, holding onto the railing with one hand and dragging his crutches with the other.

Alya and Yurgi settled down on the steps with Goldy between them.

"Well, it looks like life is still normal at your house." Max shook his head and handed me my book satchel.

"I wish we had an exciting life," Hildy said as they walked away.

"No, you don't."

"Yes, I do. Our life is boring."

"Our life is peaceful." Max arched one eyebrow.

I watched their red heads bob as they walked down the street. Right now, I agreed with Max. Peaceful sounded real nice. I tapped Yurgi and Alya on their heads but stared at Yurgi. "Can both of you take turns brushing Goldy?" They nodded together.

"Good." I squeezed between them up the steps. As I closed the door, Yurgi said, "Here, Alya, you go first." I leaned against the door to latch it and smiled to myself. I had to tell Max that Yurgi was making progress.

When I glanced up, I faced Taty and Jimmy, sitting on the bed-couch. Papa, Roy, and Marty were on straight-backed chairs. One chair was empty. Papa pointed to it. I sat.

"How were your troubles today?" Papa asked. I glanced around the room and brushed my hair from my face, stalling on how to answer.

"Not too many troubles today, Papa. Betsy behaved at Infant Socks. The teachers didn't pile on as much homework, and it's a golden fall day."

I leaned back, until I glanced at Taty's bandaged thumb. I jumped up and ran to her. "Is your infection spreading?" I carefully lifted her arm and examined the red streak.

Taty patted my hand. "Thanks to Marty's good care today, it might be a little better. I'm very grateful that it's no worse."

I laid her arm back onto her lap and took my seat.

"So, did someone call this meeting?" I asked.

"I did. I'd like to explain." Papa took a deep breath. "I have bad news. Since you're only fourteen, Mr. Luczak will not allow you to work more than a week, even if you turn fifteen soon. The law states you have to be seventeen to work in a factory."

"Great!" I jumped from my chair again. How could that be bad news? I was thrilled to be done with Infant Socks.

Taty kept her eyes down. Papa leaned toward me. "That's bad news for our family because Mr. Luczak has to fill Taty's position now. Infant Socks has too many orders to be short one cutter for a few weeks."

I sank onto my chair, regretting my short but selfish moment of happiness.

"Our whole family will suffer without Taty's income, especially since we have two extra mouths and a dog to feed." Papa smiled at our expanding family. "We're happy to have them here, but I'm not sure we can take care of everyone."

Marty clapped and jumped up. "I'm seventeen. Maybe I could work at Infant Socks and pay room and board for Jimmy and me to live here. When Taty is better, she can have her job back. After that, Roy, Jimmy, and I will figure something out."

She glanced at Roy. He grinned and pulled her beside him again. Papa studied the two of them. It wasn't quite his practicing patience look, but it was definitely his thinking look.

"Marty, I can't ask Mr. Luczak to hire you if you're not qualified," Papa said. "Do you have sewing skills?"

"She sure enough does." Jimmy straightened his shoulders. "Marty sewed all our clothes because Ma was busy with the babies and doing other people's laundry. If Marty can't sew, nobody can."

Marty put her arm around Jimmy and squeezed him until his cheeks turned pink.

Papa stood up. "That's very kind of you, Marty. Your idea is worth a try. Why don't you come along to work with Lis and me tomorrow? Mr. Luczak might just like it."

Goldy barked outside, and Yurgi slammed in the front door. "John's here with a man in a black-and-green jacket." Yurgi wrinkled his nose. "He's pretty dirty looking, but he wants to come in."

CHAPTER 44

Papa and I jumped up together. He beat me in the rush to the door and stood with his legs apart and arms crossed. I peeked from behind Papa.

"John, what's going on here?" Papa demanded.

John lifted his hands. "Pavel, I didn't bring this man here. He brought me. He stopped me on my way home and said it was time to make an appearance."

The dirty man peered at us, leaning on a thick stick. His bushy brows almost covered his eyes and a gray beard hid the rest of his face.

"Austin?" I whispered.

"I reckon you have some of my people in your house." Austin's voice rasped. "And I've come to take them home."

Marty squeezed in beside me. "Grandpa?"

Austin glanced past Papa at Marty. A smile lit his face. "There's my girl. She played the role of a hobo just fine, but isn't she a pretty young lady?"

Marty tore down the steps and into Austin's arms. They laughed and cried as they rocked in a long hug.

"You don't look like my grandpa with that scruffy beard, and your name is not Austin. What's going on here?" Marty stepped back and patted her grandpa's whiskered face.

Austin glanced at me. "Sorry to deceive you, Lester. My real name is James. I'm proud to say that little Jimmy is named for me."

I covered my mouth and giggled. "And my real name is Lis. What is going on here?"

"I was searching for my grandkids to bring them home. I had a late start that slowed me down at first. Finally, I found their trail."

Marty leaned forward. "Grandpa, we didn't leave a trail."

James's eyes crinkled in a grin. "Sometimes you track with your ears. I just had to ask. People noticed you. It was odd to see three young hobos who traveled together and kept to themselves."

James squeezed Marty's arms. "Here in Fond du Lac, I caught up to you. I was deciding how to approach you when I sprained my ankle. I could hardly walk and was afraid I'd lose you again. You can imagine how relieved I was to see you were already being looked after by some wonderful people, so I watched and waited for the perfect time."

Papa held the door open. "Why don't you come in? Lis will put on a kettle of water for tea, and we can all have a chat. Yurgi and Alya, you come in too. We're about to hear another story, a really good one."

"What about Goldy?" Yurgi stood on the sidewalk, holding Goldy's rope, staring at Papa with pleading eyes. "She's all clean from her brushing. May she come in?"

Papa sighed. "Well, alright. I wouldn't want you to miss the beginning of the story by taking Goldy to the shed, but you're responsible to keep hold of her rope."

"I will, Papa. And I'll sit by Jimmy so he can help too."

Papa and I exchanged a grin.

Marty linked arms with her grandpa and pulled him into the house. "Jimmy, look who's here."

Jimmy gripped the cushions of the bed-couch and pushed himself against the wall, back straight, face tight. "I don't want Grandpa to be here. He'll take me home to that horrible man who kicked me out. I ain't never going back."

Nobody moved but James. He took his time limping to the bed-couch and eased himself onto the edge. He folded and unfolded his hands before turning to Jimmy. "You're right. I'm ashamed of how your pa treated you. I'm ashamed he's my son. How could anybody kick out a boy of ten?"

Jimmy's nostrils flared. "Pa is crazy."

"I reckon you're right about that too." James sighed. "He was crazy with fear that your uncontrolled anger could destroy you. He was crazy with fear that his family was starving and there was nothing he could do about it. And after you and Marty ran away, he was crazy with regret that he'd never see you again to apologize."

James patted Jimmy's cast. "Your poor ma wept for days. She was caught between standing with her husband and loving you more than her own life."

Jimmy's eyes warmed. "I sure do miss my ma."

Marty sat on the other side of Jimmy. "Me too. She was the sweetness in our life of troubles."

"That she was and still is," James said. "It's because of her that I took the biggest challenge of my game-tracking history— tracking my grandchildren." He glanced at Roy. "And the kind young man who tried to keep these children safe."

"Grandpa, I'm not a child anymore." Marty stood beside Roy. "We're going to get married."

"Yes, s-s-sir," Roy stuttered. "I'd like your permission to marry your granddaughter. I love her very much and will do everything to protect her."

"You've already proven that, Roy." James stood and shook Roy's hands. "I've seen how you've sacrificed for Marty and for Jimmy. You have my blessing on your future as husband and wife. Maybe we can all head home tomorrow."

"Grandpa, there are no jobs at home. We want to stay in Fond du Lac," Marty said. "I might have a part time job, at least for now." She glanced at Taty. "Eddy has been talking to Roy about hiring him. After we're married, we can move into Eddy's house and work for him. I'd clean and cook. Roy would do upkeep on the house, getting it ready for Eddy's bride."

"Eddy's bride?" Papa raised an eyebrow and stared at me.

"The new Eddy," I whispered.

Jimmy scooted forward. "What about me? Who wants me?"

Goldy stretched and licked Jimmy's cheek.

CHAPTER 45

A horn tooted outside. Yurgi ran to the window. "It's Albert and Heinrich. I don't believe it. Albert's driving Heinrich's old truck."

John hurried to the window and stared over Yurgi's head. "What's he doing driving Heinrich's truck?"

Albert grinned toward the window and tooted the horn again, waving for us to come out.

James hugged Jimmy. "I'll stay here with my dear grandson."

Roy held Marty's hand. "We'll stay here, too."

"I'll keep them company," Taty said.

The rest of us rushed to the street. John stuck his head in the truck's open window, frowning at Albert. "What's happening here? I thought we were buying an old automobile together."

Heinrich leaned forward, peering over Albert's hands, gripping the steering wheel. "Settle down, John. Albert and I have worked out a deal, but it won't work at all without you."

"John, my friend," Albert said, "I couldn't buy an automobile or even this rundown truck without you."

"Rundown truck?" Heinrich sputtered. "Excuse me, young man. This well-used truck might be old, but it's a gem."

"Don't gems sparkle?" Papa joined the conversation. "Not much sparkle in rust."

"Her sparkle is within." Heinrich leaned back with a humph.

Albert scooted from the car and trotted to John. "Heinrich has offered us his gem of a truck." He glanced over his shoulder at Heinrich. "Just to rent for now."

Heinrich crawled out of the passenger side and leaned on the hood. "Since my hours on the railroad have been cut, sweet Rachel and I are running short on cash. The rent money will help with our expenses."

Albert nodded. "And the truck will take us all over town. I can drive you to work at Sadoffs and then zip around with my deliveries."

John's eyes narrowed.

"I'll be able to deliver bigger items and even double my business. Think how much easier it will be when winter arrives."

John chewed on his lip.

Albert lifted his hands. "Well? Do you like the deal?"

John laughed and spun Albert around. "Of course I like the deal. I love the deal. When can I drive?"

Heinrich sat in the passenger seat. "Right now, son. Get in."

I ran around to Heinrich's window. "May I come along?"

"We better wait until John has a lesson or two," Heinrich said. "Not everyone catches onto the skill of shifting, braking, hitting the gas, and steering." Heinrich's eyes twinkled as he peered out at Papa. "Right, Pavel?"

Papa crossed his arms. "I had hoped you had forgotten that day. I haven't tried to drive an automobile since."

"How could I forget that near-death experience with you behind the wheel, bumping down the railroad tracks instead of the road?" Heinrich slapped his knee and laughed. "Now, if you all will please step back, let's see if John can handle this gem."

"Having this truck will be wonderful." John yelled out the window, patted the steering wheel, and then turned his attention to Heinrich's instructions.

Papa herded us to the front steps just as the old truck jerked forward and stalled. John flashed an apologetic smile. "I'll get this." Again, it jerked forward and stalled.

Albert cupped his hands to his mouth and shouted. "It will be wonderful if you ever learn to drive."

John shrugged then grabbed the steering wheel as the truck took off, heading for the railroad tracks.

CHAPTER 46

The gem of a truck with John and Heinrich inside swerved back onto Brooke Street and out of sight. "Well, I guess the show is over." Chuckling, Papa headed toward the front steps. "Albert and John will be good drivers. Maybe I should get another lesson."

I grabbed Papa's arm. "No, you had a lesson a couple years ago. Driving is not for you. Remember? Walking is safer and good for your health. But driving might be for me. Albert said he'd teach me."

"I did not," Albert said.

"Then it was John." I turned and blocked Albert's next step.

He shook his head, eyes sparkling. "It wasn't John either. He said driving automobiles is not for girls."

I crossed my arms. "Well, I see that I'm going to have to change a few minds."

We were all laughing as we tramped into the living room. James stood. "It's time for a family meeting."

Yurgi tugged on Papa's jacket. "Is it time for another prayer meeting?"

"Who said prayer meeting?" James scratched his ear.

Alya stared up at James. "Sometimes when we have important things to talk about, we start with a prayer."

"Well, I'll be. How did my young'uns find the door of such a fine Christian family?" James asked.

"God planned it, Grandpa," Jimmy said.

"I do believe you're right, son. Yep, it's time for a prayer meeting because we have big things to talk about. Pavel, will you lead us in prayer?"

We scrambled to find chairs. When Papa bowed his head, so did we. "Dear Lord, Your ways are not our ways. Sometimes our troubles seem more than we can bear and yet You are always with us, planning our paths, showing Your love. We can hardly understand all the steps You took to bring us together on this day. Bless Marty and Roy as they look forward to their married life. Show Jimmy that he is loved by many people and especially by You. Help our family to be a blessing to everyone here. In Jesus' name we pray. Amen."

Goldy barked once. "That's her amen, Papa." Yurgi giggled and gave Goldy a hug.

"Thank you for that beautiful prayer, Pavel." James wiped his eyes and stood again. "While you were outside, my family, with the help of Taty, discussed our plans. Taty, you go first."

Taty cleared her throat. "We should host Marty and Roy's wedding in our living room. Soon. Since I'm home from work for awhile yet, I could plan the meal. The girls will help, and Frau Brunhild and Rachel will want to be included too."

Roy smiled at Marty. "But it will be soon. Maybe a week from Saturday. I have always respected Marty, but other people might not believe that. This is the right thing to do."

"Yes siree, soon is best," Jimmy said. "After the wedding, I'm going to go back with Grandpa to see my sweet ma and give Pa a chance to say he's sorry. Maybe I'll tell him I'm sorry too."

James gave Jimmy a hug and pulled Marty in for a bigger one. "Of course, I want to be here to give my beautiful granddaughter to a wonderful young man." James blinked. "And Jimmy and I can still hop a train to West Virginia before the snow flies."

I lifted my hands. "How did this happen? I stepped out the door to watch John get a driving lesson, and while we were out there, you all planned a wedding. Without me."

"And without me." Papa stepped forward, frowning. "Don't I have some say in this?"

Taty and Marty glanced at each other, grinning. Taty reached for my hand and smiled at Papa. "Marty and I chatted about it earlier, even agreed that the wedding should be soon. Now with James here, it seems perfect."

Papa's shoulders relaxed. "Well actually, it's a very good idea. Getting married is the proper thing to do." He rubbed his hands together, glancing into the corner where his violin rested. "And I can tune up my violin. It's been too long since we've had music in this house. I'll ask Heinrich to bring his stumpf fiddle too."

"Stumpf fiddle?" Marty asked.

Papa winked. "You'll see."

Marty grinned and grabbed my hand. "We want you and John to be our witnesses. You both did so much for us."

I clapped. "I've never been in a wedding."

"What about me?" Albert plopped down on the nearest chair. "I led the search with Albert's Soup Saturday."

Roy glanced at Marty. She nodded. Roy stepped up to Albert. "You're right. We want all three of you to be our witnesses."

I nudged Albert's elbow. "Still getting things done."

"Yep." He blushed.

Jimmy tapped my hand. I knelt in front of him. "And you're ready to go home and give it another try?"

"Yep. Grandpa convinced me that Pa has changed, and Ma will hug me to pieces. The whole family will love Goldy."

Yurgi hopped up. "Goldy can't go. She's mine."

CHAPTER 47

——•—••—•—••—•——

Saturday – A week later

The week before the wedding zoomed by. Marty worked at Infant Socks. I returned to school fulltime. Taty, Frau Brunhild, and Rachel planned the menu during the first days of the week then hustled around our kitchen baking cakes and cookies, ham and potatoes. On Friday, Eddy invited Roy and Marty, Albert, John, and me to his house to find wedding clothes in his well-stocked closets. Papa and Heinrich hauled in extra benches and set them up in our living room. By Saturday evening, all was ready.

While Marty and I dressed in our room, John, Albert, and Roy got ready in Papa and Taty's room.

I braided Marty's long, blonde hair into a single strand, then I wrapped it around her head, pinned it into a crown, and tucked marigolds around it. I stepped back to admire her. "Beautiful."

Marty's dark eyes crinkled into a sparkly smile.

"May we come in?" Taty knocked and peered around the door. "You both are so pretty already, but Rachel has something to add."

The two of them waltzed in, carrying colorful shoulder bouquets. "I cut these mums and marigolds before the frost," Rachel said. She pinned the bouquet of yellow, gold, and deep-red flowers onto Marty's shoulder then held her at arms' length. "This is perfect with your dark, rose-colored dress."

Marty inhaled the fragrance of the fall flowers as tears welled in her eyes. "I can't believe how kind you all have been. I've changed from a runaway hobo to beautiful bride in only a couple of weeks."

"Helping you has brought us nothing but joy." Taty gave her a careful hug. "And quite a bit of stress."

We laughed together.

"You're next," Taty said, as Rachel pinned a similar bouquet on my shoulder, only mine had more yellows and golds. "This is just the color you needed on your navy-blue dress."

Marty grabbed me by the hands, twirling me around in a happy dance, while Rachel and Taty clapped.

A lively tune bounced through the door. "Oh, it's Papa's violin!" I clapped to the rhythm.

Taty nodded, her eyes sparkling. "Beautiful, isn't it?"

As the music faded away, a clatter replaced it. "What's that other racket?" I asked. "It sounds like drums and bells and tin cans banging."

Rachel's dimples deepened. "That's Heinrich and his stumpf fiddle to add to the noise. I mean, celebration. And I think it's your Papa clapping along."

Taty giggled. "They're up to mischief again."

The noise stopped and Yurgi yelled through the door, "It's time." Taty and Rachel gave us each another hug and slipped from the room to find their seats.

Marty touched my arm, her eyes serious. "I need a short prayer meeting. Will you say a prayer for Roy and me?"

I held her hands. "Dear Lord, thank You for the love You have given to Marty and Roy. Please guide them as they begin their lives as husband and wife. We know that You have plans to prosper them, to give them hope and a future. Bless their marriage with happiness." I squeezed Marty's hands tighter and giggled. "And lots of children. In Jesus' name we pray. Amen."

Marty's eyes opened wide. "Lis!"

The stumpf fiddle racket ended. Only the sweet melody of Papa's violin floated through the air.

Yurgi swung the door open wide and bowed. "It's really time."

As I stepped from our bedroom, Yurgi skipped over to sit with Taty, Alya, and Jimmy. Goldy sat at their feet with a red ribbon around her neck. James waited by the door. Smiling faces turned toward me, faces of our friends—Frau Brunhild, Max and Hildy, Rachel and Heinrich, Eddy and Miss Meuschlin, and even Officer Kowalski, plus Doris and Betsy from Infant Socks.

At the far side of the living room, Albert and John stood on one side of Pastor Siefert, Roy on the other. The young men, decked out in Eddy's dark suits, white shirts, and ties, their hair slicked back, waited with folded hands.

The tune of "Amazing Grace" floated from Papa's violin. That was my cue to stroll forward, but my knees shook. My feet refused to take the short walk to where they waited by the front window. The seriousness of the moment hit me.

"It's time," Marty whispered behind me, standing in the doorway. She gave me a nudge. I was frozen. John fidgeted with his sleeve and glanced at Jimmy. But Albert, my bossy, dear friend, with a slight movement of his hand, motioned me forward, and my fear melted.

I walked toward Albert, confident again, and took my place beside him. As Marty glided forward on the arm of her grandpa, the golden sunset lit our living room. Roy's eyes glistened with tears, and Marty blushed.

CHAPTER 48

Sunday

Sunday was always my favorite day of the week, but not this one. This afternoon, the day after the wedding, Papa, Taty, Alya, Yurgi, Goldy and I waited on our front steps. We were going to say goodbye to James and Jimmy, but we were giving the family a few moments together.

Roy and Marty stood in the front yard with Jimmy and James. Roy had his arm around Jimmy, while Marty sobbed into her grandpa's shoulder. "I know I belong here with Roy." She grabbed Roy's hand. "I want to be here with Roy, but part of my heart wants to go home with you too."

James patted her shaking shoulders. "Good-byes are always hard, but you have a wonderful new life here with Roy. Everyone can see that you love each other very much. Jimmy and I must head home to your ma and pa. That's where we belong. This is where you belong."

Marty smiled through her tears and stepped back. She tugged on Jimmy's arm, trying to pull him into their embrace. Instead he tripped on a crutch and fell into her.

"Whoa, Marty, don't break my other leg."

She caught him in a tight hug and, laughing, squeezed him tighter. "You be sure to pass this hug on to Ma and Pa and all the babies." She kissed his cheek before he could pull away. "And don't you wipe that kiss off." He did, but his eyes twinkled.

When Eddy and Miss Meuschlin pulled up, the rest of us clambered off the steps and into the good-byes. Hand shaking, hugging, laughing, crying, and lots of barking all happened at once.

"Goldy, what's wrong?" Yurgi kneeled and petted her head. "Why are you barking?" He clung to Goldy's rope.

Jimmy swung closer on his crutches. "I think she wants to go with me."

"No, she doesn't. She's my dog." Tears gathered in Yurgi's eyes as he pulled Goldy closer.

"We should let her pick." Jimmy stooped down to pet Goldy. She turned her head back and forth, focusing on one boy and then the other.

I squatted in front of Goldy and scratched behind her ears. "Dear Goldy, you are a lucky dog to be loved so much by two little boys. What do you want, girl?"

Goldy studied me with her big brown eyes. I coaxed her rope from Yurgi and led her toward the house. When I sat on a step, she settled herself at my feet, staring at me. The boys followed along. Both planted themselves in front of me with unblinking, sad eyes.

Now I had three sets of eyes staring at me. I closed mine to think. When I opened them, Papa and James stood there, studying me too.

"I s'pose we could bring Goldy on the train." James lifted one shoulder.

"Grandpa, really?" Jimmy spun to look at him. "I would take good care of her."

Papa ruffled Yurgi's hair. "I'm not sure that's such a good idea, James. Goldy already thinks of this as her home. We love her."

"I love her," I whispered.

"I really love her!" Yurgi twisted to look at Papa and folded his hands in a silent plea.

For a moment, no one said anything. Eddy broke the silence. "Well, let's get going." He opened the back door of his automobile. "I didn't buy your tickets to West Virginia for you to miss the train."

James sighed. "C'mon, son. We must show our gratitude to Eddy and move along. Goldy has a good home here."

Jimmy kissed Goldy's head. "Now don't you wipe that off." He brushed a tear from his cheek and headed toward the open door. As he pulled himself into the automobile, Goldy yanked free and bounded toward him.

"No!" Yurgi shouted and fell into a sobbing heap.

I held my breath. Goldy picked up a mitten that had dropped from Jimmy's pocket and held it in her teeth for Jimmy. "Well, thank you, Goldy." He petted her head. "You wanna come along?"

Goldy's tail wagged, but she spun around and trotted back to me. I grabbed her rope and scratched her ears. "Yurgi, get up. Looks like Goldy made her choice. She picked me."

Yurgi lifted his tear-stained face. Goldy licked his tears. "I think she picked us, Lis." He hugged Goldy and me.

Before Eddy closed the door, Jimmy called, "Hey, Yurgi, thanks for being my friend. Take good care of our dog."